OUTSIDE THE BONES

OUTSIDE THE BONES

Lyn Di Iorio

Arte Público Press
Houston, Texas

Outside the Bones is made possible in part from grants from the city of Houston through the Houston Arts Alliance.

Recovering the past, creating the future

Arte Público Press
University of Houston
452 Cullen Performance Hall
Houston, Texas 77204-2004

Cover art by Wilfred Santiago
Cover design by Mora Des!gn

Di Iorio, Lyn
    Outside the Bones / by Lyn Di Iorio.
        p. cm.
    ISBN 978-1-55885-703-2 (alk. paper)
        1. Witches—Fiction. 2. Witchcraft—Fiction. 3. Blessing and cursing—Fiction. 4. Spirits—Fiction. 5. Missing persons—Fiction. 6. New York (N.Y.)—Fiction. 7. Puerto Rico—Fiction. I. Title.
    PS3604.I115O98 2011
    813'.6—dc22

                                                      2011025356
                                                            CIP

♾ The paper used in this publication meets the requirements of the American National Standard for Information Sciences—Permanence of Paper for Printed Library Materials, ANSI Z39.48-1984.

11 12 13 14 15 16 17   10 9 8 7 6 5 4 3 2 1

Where are the songs I used to know?
Where are the notes I used to sing?
I have forgotten everything
I used to know so long ago.

Christina Rossetti

Elena era muy preciosa,
era la reina del arrabal,
y ese malvado por celos,
que su carita vino a cortar.

Puerto Rican plena

Nsambia says, but *Palo* does,
For good, and also for evil.

Tata Victor Tumba Fuego,
Master of Fire

CONTENTS

For Xavier

You are everything. Para siempre.

PART ONE

ONE
AN ACCIDENTAL *FUFÚ*

Somebody else walking past homeboy on Broadway in the summer wouldn't glance twice at him. Even if he was wearing his flamingo dupioni shirt, as pink and textured as a tongue. To somebody else, he would be just another light-brown man with raisin-clumped hair already starting to gray in the sideburns. Three buttons on the sticky shirt unbuttoned. A Santa Bárbara medallion and a gold baby shoe in his chest hair. He was just one more Hispanic male up on the West Side of the isle of Manhattan, height and weight and features all measured by statistics.

But to me, he was a nice-talking, sweet-walking fine *puto* of a Puerto Rican, a guy that spoke to me of men in white shirts and straw hats dancing *bomba*, of palms and mangroves on a regal island that never was. I found him so goddamn irresistible I thought all other women did too, even his daughter that wasn't his daughter.

It's that musician thing. I have, or used to have, a thing for them, the ones that play so sweet it's like they got you in their high and in their hell, all caught up in a net woven by a thousand threads of melody. The thing makes me see something different from what the guy is. It's like I suddenly see what the guy wants to be or what he could be or what I could be if I let his music take me the way it lifts him. It's like I'm what they call *montada*. Possessed. Not by the man but by his music, like his music is more spirit than music. That made sense to me back then because although I pretended to be a witch, and I was

1

hungry for the unseen to manifest itself to me, in me, it never really had.

My spirit working was more about what people wanted it to be. I was good at making people believe they'd get what they wanted with a little pinch of honey, splashes of Florida water, a ground up tiger's nail from Perla's Botánica thrown over a photo and penciled paper. Yeah, focus their anxieties with the chaos of my creation. Whenever I did a *trabajito,* a *fufú,* people in the hood believed it would work for them. They'd trade in kind, clean my house, get me concert tickets and buy me gift coupons to my favorite Italian restaurants. Life can be comfortable when you got a lot of people's faith behind you. What they believe creates a current; and that current becomes their reality.

But I was still hungry for a spirit that could touch me too.

Maybe music was the god or spirit world that I was looking for.

I was on the tail end of my marriage. My husband Gus was a bus driver, a nice white guy. I think I may have married him because when I was in my twenties his being white and even-tempered seemed to guarantee that he would always be nice. He didn't like it that I called him "white" though. Irish American. Safe. Then.

And then the realization. He slept with another chick. I found out because she called to tell me one afternoon in broken English and a chirpy voice that maybe made Gus dream of pagodas, red silk unfurling, a sinuous great wall winding ever closer, about to wall the motherfucker in his tomb. Anyway, after Gus got back from his shift, I chest bumped him into a corner. I can do that, for I am a big girl. Usually if I move too quick in streets and stores, that's enough for people—the roughest, readiest New Yorkers—to fly out of my way.

Plaster cracked under his head, and he gasped.

"Am I losing my exotic appeal?"

"What?"

I breathed out coffee fumes. "I hear you eating Chinese pussy these days."

He tried to look away, and he didn't say nothing.

"¡*Pendejo!*" I grabbed him by both shoulders and tried to lift him up against the wall. I couldn't do it, but it was, as they say, a brave effort. He was, at least, trapped.

"Fina, can you stop smashing my windpipe?" He coughed. "Please."

I pulled my loaf-like arms away, and his feet went flat on the floor. "Why?"

His eyes passed over my long-beaded extensions, which made a rich sound when I moved, like change in my pocket.

"She was different." His head-to-toe went on. He glanced at the tattooed lovebirds spilling out of my stretchy low-cut top, and finally stopped at the jelly belly that didn't like to stay under nothing. "You know, thin."

I yelled, "I'll find my own exotic lover!" And then I pushed my fist through the wall. Or maybe I punched and then yelled, but Gus was ready this time, and he ducked. The pain as if my knuckle bones had been pulverized was a great distraction for me.

I ranted about how he could fly off to China with his little geisha girl and leave me alone. And don't think I'm an ignorant fuck, I know geishas aren't Chinese, but I was trying to make a point.

Gus ran out of the apartment, and spent the night out. I walked up and down the apartment, real annoyed that my boxing hand was hurt and I couldn't punch at the wall again. But then I started to realize that my hand was hurt worse than my heart.

The truth was that after I had started learning *Palo Monte* about a year or so ago, Gus and I had been spending less and less time together. Gus' reaction to *Palo* was, "That stuff freaks me out, man." And somehow, even though I was real drawn to *Palo*, I always felt as if Gus' baby blues were watching me when I came back from Tata Victor's apartment. Judging. Holding me back.

So it was a relief that I wouldn't have to be held back no more. But I felt bad that I felt good, if that makes any sense.

It ain't so easy to break up with eleven years. The next day Gus brought plaster, paint and purple tulips, which we both thought I liked. He said he had told Chirpy to take a hike.

I didn't look him in the eye, but I accepted the tulips with the hand that wasn't bandaged. I pressed them to my nose. Tulips have a deep green smell, which I appreciate. I may be a big girl, but I have a refined soul.

A week later when he was out driving the bus, I saw flyers posted on the bulletin board in our building lobby next to the laminated sheet with contact numbers for the 24th precinct.

There was a photo shop picture of Chico, my upstairs neighbor, back arched like a windblown sapling. He was blowing into his trumpet, and his eyes were closed like he was praying.

I didn't know him real well, just from his rushed "Hey, Fina!" as he flew down our building's front steps in his clown-bright clothes. Sometimes the bumping of his trumpet and flute cases on the floors in the apartment above woke me from dreams of thunder hitting the zinc-roofed shack of my childhood. My waking screams prompted Gus to say that the music cases had to be Chico's front for a deeper passion, which involved the carting around of body parts.

Below the picture:

ESCAPE TO THE COPA,
THE RENOWNED COPACABANA! 563 W. 34th St.
WHERE CHICO
ENCHANTS LOVERS
OF SALSA AND BOLERO

And just like that, I suddenly didn't like tulips or that mortuary shade of purple.

Chico was standing in green track lighting way in front of the band, next to the singer, a bald guy in white satin whose *voz de vieja* couldn't compete with Chico's trumpet, which trilled as clear as crystal breaking; and then broke into a freer, jazzier web over the beating of the congas.

A man whose face I barely saw grabbed hold of my waist and spun me into the sea of dancers. The music lassoed me out of my fat girl avatar and into sweaty J.Lo turns against my faceless partner's jeans. I danced to a solo sharp as the blue of the skies over El Combate beach, and then one where I was falling, falling, falling into the black water of the Puerto Rico trench. I finally noticed that the thin guy was slapping my butt after every turn, and trying to lick my lovebirds. Worse: he had a pizza face, so I skipped to the ladies' room.

On my way back, I stopped by the bandstand. The music was taking Chico to a place I wanted to go. He was like a cherub with a piccolo, a child starting or ending the world with melody. I could barely stand the way his lips—plump, tender *bembas*—kissed the trumpet and his fingers, like pieces of sticky caramel, caressed the stops as he leaned back, almost overcome. And that made the women come over to the bandstand, panting.

Now a lot of men I know have rear ends as hard as a *chayote*, but Chico de León had real manners to boot. Not only did he sign fifty autographs, he chatted up most of the *fanaticada* that night, even some old lady wrapped from head to toe in black like the Reaper. He didn't seem to favor the younger girls flashing raccoon eyes and winking cleavage.

I did this myself, I admit. When he hugged me, I let my lovebirds peck at him.

He pulled back, and introduced me to a red-haired groupie with flowered press-ons shooting to Guinness fame. "Hey, this is my neighbor, Fina. She's a musician of magic, like I'm a magician of music."

"How'd you know I'm a . . . musician of magic?"

"Everybody knows that about you, just like they know about me."

One of my extensions was hanging over my cheek, and he pushed it behind my ear. Gus hadn't done that in. . . . Had he ever done that? It worked on me: warmth flooded me from chest to booty.

I pulled out the new Canon that Gus had bought me for my birthday and waved it at him, muttering something about how my best friend liked his playing.

Chico's warm fingers curled around my wrist. "Don't you put no *fufús* on me, Doña Fina, not for anybody, I don't care how much they beg you. I've had enough of people taking pieces off my shirt and spitting on them. I ain't got the time to make that shit bounce back."

"I won't do no harm," I said. "I'll guard it with my life." Then I took his picture like I was taking his soul.

I printed the picture and put it away. I guess cheaters expect their partners to cheat too because Gus started rooting around in my drawer where I kept our birth certificates and passports. He found the picture, waved it under my nose. "I knew you were starting to go sweet on somebody. Can't believe it's that serial killer *conguero*!"

"He's not a *conguero*."

Gus burned the picture over the stovetop.

It still hurts me to think that I was somehow responsible for what happened to poor Chico. That was the day of the night he went off to play, with a high color in his cheeks, which I mistakenly ascribed to rum and the fact that the Tito Puente Orchestra was featuring him, and he collapsed on the stage right after his solo.

Malanga the ancient Havana *conguero*, who lived upstairs across from Chico, came down the next day and told us what happened. Chico tried to get up after his last solo, but fell back into a sitting position.

The women swarmed the stage and the musicians practically had to yank the feverish Chico out of his jacket and pants, which the women were tearing off his body. A young thing dressed in a black cat suit and wearing one of them spiked Goth collars bit into his hand. One house-sized Latina shouted

"Gonna save you, Papi," and jumped on both him and the Goth girl.

Then Chico disappeared under the pullulating hill of fat and thin, fly and fugly, sequinned and bejeanned, only his face visible. A photographer took pictures. It took three musicians and two security guards to pull him out. When they did, he was covered with mouth-sized hearts all over his naked arms and torso.

He went to the hospital, and it turned out he had pneumonia and a stomach obstruction. The doctors couldn't cure him for a long time, probably because with so many scraps of his clothing stuck beneath candles, in honey, under water and inside coconuts; or tied up with yarn, hair and money; or sprinkled with blood, gunpowder, sugar, spit and God knows what else, poor Chico's body didn't know if it was being cursed or blessed.

But there was a good side to this accidental *fufú*: Gus said that finding the picture showed him that the two of us were like Sigourney Weaver and the chest-bursting bug, so he was going on vacation to China to think things over.

I didn't need to go on no vacation: I just changed the locks on the door.

Chico got back from the hospital on a Saturday afternoon, and within minutes I shot upstairs with a restorative *caldo*. He opened the door in striped pajamas, his eyes puffy, his skin as pale as brown skin can get. When I offered him the container of soup, he hesitated at first, probably scared of more *fufús*.

But he was even more impressed by my Great Dane enthusiasms. We sat down at his spindly table, and he passed a hand over the stubble on his chin. "Hell if I know what happened that night with the Tito Puente orchestra."

I muttered something about how he should go easy on the rum.

"Time was when I didn't have to drink or do lines to get revved." He shrugged. "But that was fifteen years back. On the island."

I myself had hazy childhood memories of the island. I imagined Chico facing the ocean, making the waves mount higher and higher to the tune of his horn.

"Why'd you leave?"

His eyes got beady, his lips pouty and an invisible Linus cloud formed over his head. "I had to. One of those island oligarchs had his thugs run me out. Nearly killed my ass."

"My bad. If you don't want. . . . "

"I ended up losing my wife." He looked away and stared into space. "Of course, I deserved that. For fucking around on her." The Linus cloud was making him hunch over. "My beautiful wife. . . . "

"Wife?"

"Long time ago. My ex," he said quickly. "She had a baby. My daughter Hilesca. They both came down with a bad fever. This was in the '90s. Shouldn't have been that way."

"My mother died of purpureal fever in 1977. Those hospitals out on the island. . . . " I shook my head.

"That's it, purpureal fever. That's what she had."

Chico had rented a *carro público* and taken his wife and baby to a private San Juan clinic. He looked for high-paying jobs. But he was poor, a kid with no connections. Worse, he was from some barrio nobody had ever heard of out on the island. In order to pay the bills, he took up gardening full-time in the rich suburbs of San Francisco and Garden Hills, and still did his gigs at night.

At first, he liked gardening because of the exercise and the time to think. Not that homeboy was a great thinker. He said something about the wind and the trees and tried to tie that to some idea of how jazz sounds are born from the breeze—it was musician's bull, and I had to bite my lip not to laugh.

"Okay, Fina, how's this?" he said. "I was bending over a hibiscus bush in this big old garden. The breeze was in my ears,

and then outta nowhere I feel a hand grab me. This woman—
she goosed me real hard."

"She" was the mistress of the house as it turned out. A senator's wife and a former Miss Universe, one with a degree from
a college in Massachusetts; and she was too tongue-tied to just
make the usual advances! All you need to do to let a man know
that you favor him is stare him in the eye and invite him in for
a big plate of rice and beans and steak. When's he's stuffed, give
him an India beer and a flan—a sweet coconut flan is the best
for awakening love.

If he can stand up from the meal, you don't need to be a
200-pound ghetto bitch queen like me to steer his grogginess
to the bed. He'll just collapse, I guarantee it. The rest is easy.

Maybe the senator's wife didn't have the time to ask her
maid to cook some rice and beans. She had seen Chico play,
and for her that was foreplay. The way he closed his eyes when
his lips caressed the trumpet made her think he could take a
woman with him to the same place he went when he wrestled
with demons. And when she saw him trimming each little leaf
so carefully, she imagined him fingering his horn. She was seeing how careful a lover of the music he was, how he could turn
air and saliva into heaven and earth by lightly feathering mouth
and fingers against surfaces: metals, flowers, a woman.

Or maybe she was just a repressed *blanquita*, a nasty horny
white girl, tired of the senator's misfiring hose and looking for
a real man. I couldn't decide.

Chico spun around and stared as she unzipped his pants,
and his instrument floated high into the air. The woman
tongued him, keeping time as she moved her head from side to
side. For weeks, she dismissed her staff, and she and Chico
played inspired rhythms in different parts of the mansion and
its grounds.

One day, she had just finished blowing a *bolero*-like rhythm
with a sudden finish. Chico told me, "Fina, she told me to just
pull up my pants, and then went into the house."

He shook his head. "But I just stood there, Fina. Miss Universe had just gone down on me, and all I could think was 'Wow!'"

And it was because Chico was so much like a boy jumping into sunlit puddles that things got bad. Out of nowhere, Miss Universe's husband walked into the patio, home for a late lunch before going back to the Capitol, and what did he see but some jerk hosing off his *pinga* in the garden.

Well, the senator was a known womanizer, and suspicious like all *mujeriegos*, what did he think but "My wife is a whore."

"I ran out of the house through an opening in the wall she had told me about," Chico said. "Then I hid out in Llorens Torres. But Senator Ferrera's thugs looked for me even in the fucking projects. Found me, beat me up real bad. I lost both of those beautiful women. Miss Universe. And my wife. . . . "

He stopped talking and swallowed.

The sunlight slanted through the kitchen window and the medallion and the baby shoe charm dazzled my eyes.

"My daughter died, Fina." He grabbed the baby shoe charm on his chest. "While I was fooling around in the garden with Miss Universe."

Hell if I know why charms and a chain glinting like that on a man's chest can be so sexy to me.

TWO
THE GIRL FROM SOMEWHERE

I knocked on Chico's apartment door. I heard a shrieky laugh and then his shout, "Come in."

What did I see when I walked into the dining area but this teenager planted on his lap. Maybe that's not so bad, but she was real developed for her age, with a chest to be proud of. She was wearing one of those leotard things, a white one so that her dark nipples showed clearly and her big ass was spread out like the Pillsbury Doughboy's in tight white shorts.

Chico shifted a little in the chair under her weight. He got all round-eyed and tight-lipped and arched an eyebrow at me.

"Doña Fina, this is Hilesca. She's . . . my daughter." Winking and blinking. "My daughter."

The only one who was down with this lie, or seemed to be, was the girl herself. She flashed a gleaming smile.

My head hitched back and forth like a pigeon's. "You're kidding! I thought you said . . . "

Then his eyebrows jumped, and he pointed his chin at the girl. She turned around to look at his face, and her forehead smashed into his jaw. He cried out "¡Ayayay!" and flew up from his chair, dumping her ass on the floor at his feet.

The girl sprang to her feet, and Chico rubbed his jaw, blinked a few times and sat back down on the dinette chair.

"Hilesca, this is Doña Fina, she's a good friend."

The girl tried to sit on his lap again, but he pushed her away like a cat and she ended up sitting on another dinette chair, glaring at me.

Even if he hadn't just the other day told me that Hilesca was dead, I wouldn't have believed she was his kid. Girl didn't look like him at all. With her Ivory-soap skin, eyes like melted black wax, werewolf eyebrows and little rosebud mouth, she was an ugly version of Betty Boop. And she was sitting there wide and shameless in those shiny white shorts.

"I'm a spirit worker," I said, swinging my beaded extensions over my shoulders. "So don't be bad." I reached over and gave her hair a little friendly tug. "You must take after your mami."

"*Uuuy,*" she said, swatting my hand away, "don't you put a *fufú* on me."

I didn't answer that, just whumped my hips against the kitchen table, and let her fret all she wanted about *fufús* and whatnot.

"Don't worry, *nena,*" Chico said. "Fina only does the good work." I nodded all innocent-like, repeating the habitual response in my mind: You can't do the good work, after all, unless there's a bad spirit to work with.

The girl pushed out her bottom lip, and shot me die-evil-bitch-die looks.

Chico looked pained, but also distracted, like all of a sudden he wanted to be wherever the music in his brain was calling him.

I didn't know what the fuck else to say. "You ain't his daughter unless you're a frigging ghost" did come to mind. So, I said I had eyes of newt and toes of frog downstairs on the burner and needed to get back.

"Eyes of what?" said the girl.

I smiled—real happy she seemed kind of stupid. Or maybe she was just playing at stupid. If that was the case, she was magnificent.

Chico got up quickly, and by the time I was on the threshold, he was next to me. He closed the apartment door behind him. "I know you think this is strange, but I gotta play along. She saw me in the paper from when the women attacked me.

Claims she's Hilesca de León. I gotta figure out what's going on with her."

I squinted. "Why the hell? You ain't sure whether your kid really died, that it?" I had a thought that wasn't pretty. "Or is it that you think she may be some other kid of yours you didn't know about?"

I was getting ready to let fly a big backhanded Judgment-Day-slap, when Chico said real quick, "My girl is dead for real, Fina, but this kid knows a lot of stuff about her. I just don't know how she knows." He licked his lips. "Somehow, I don't think telling her I'm on to her is going to help me figure out what she's up to."

"Little heifer shows up telling you she's your dead kid, and you don't slap her silly? Next thing you know she'll be asking you for child support back pay."

Chico laughed. "She's out of luck on that one. My riches are in my talent." Chico puckered his lips so they looked even meatier. "I'm not gonna confront her just yet. One thing's for sure. Whatever she wants from me, she wants bad enough to put on the show of her life." He shrugged. "In principal, I'm not against that."

"What does she say she knows?"

He grabbed my arm. "She knows little shit. Stuff that on its own anybody could know." He breathed out and shook his head. "Problem is: she knows a helluva lot of little shit. She knows that the name 'Hilesca' is made up of the first syllables of the names of my dead family: my ma Hilda, my pop Esteban and my brother Carlos."

I folded my arms across my chest. He went on. The girl knew that Chico's ex's name was Aurora, and that Aurora's sister was named Jahaira. She knew that Jahaira had a gold tooth and was tall with almost night-black skin, rare for Puerto Rico.

"She could know Jahaira from anywhere, and Jahaira could have told her the . . . little shit," I suggested.

He nodded quickly. "Sure. Question is why?"

Chico's voice got squeakier, and he started waving his hands around a lot. The girl had described the raw-boarded wooden *casita* in Loíza Aldea, which belonged to Aurora's family.

"She says she remembers that it was built on stilts. And that it was close to where the river meets the sea. That's exactly where it was! Exactly!" He touched both my shoulders with both his hands, and his nostrils flared. "She remembers seeing it when she was a baby."

"So she saw it when she was a baby. Again, this Jahaira could have taken her there, or just told her about it. Maybe she's Jahaira's daughter. Or, you know, she met Jahaira somehow."

He took his hands off my shoulders. "She told me something I never heard, but which doesn't surprise me at all. She says Jahaira told her Aurora walked off into the sunset sixteen years ago, and nobody knows what happened to her."

"What happened?" And how could Chico not know? But I didn't want to make him pissy by asking too many questions. Didn't his telling me all this shit mean that he liked me? I let him talk.

The day after Chico fled the Ferrera mansion, he found a safe place to stay with another musician who lived in the Llorens Torres projects. He called Aurora at the private hospital, but the nurse who answered the phone told him that mother and child had been discharged. After calling over and over again for the next twenty-four hours, he finally got Aurora on the phone at their little house close to Toro Negro.

"Aurorita, I need to see you and the *nena*. But I'm in trouble, so I can't be there until tomorrow."

Through the static on the lousy phone, he heard Aurora's voice echo, "We have nothing, nothing, nothing. To talk talk talk about."

The thought hit him that she knew about the affair, and his knees buckled. "But I need to see my little girl."

"You piece of shit *cabrón*! Fucking around with a married woman. Well, you know what? Miss *Puta*'s husband canceled all the checks for the hospital! You fucked another woman while our daughter was dying. Dying, *hijo de puta*! And dead. You hear me, *canto de cabrón*. She's dead, and it's your fault."

"Dead? How?"

"The *carro público* stopped, and I got out, and she was fucking dead in my arms." Then it was Aurora's jagged sobs he heard, and static and a refrain of "my arms, my arms, my arms."

Aurora's breath crackled in his ears. "You motherfucking *hijo de puta chocha*-lipped *culo*-headed, *cabrón*. I hope that Senator Ferrera and his thugs catch you and feed you to the sharks off Piñones!"

"That's nothing compared to what I feel should happen to me."

"You deserve to feel that way," she sobbed.

He went back to Toro Negro. First, he visited the baby's grave in the barrio cemetery, and then he called Aurora from a pay phone and told her he was coming home. "You can take a knife and stab me," he said.

He heard laughter through the static. "You think you deserve the energy it would take me to stab you?"

When he got to their zinc-roofed house, Aurora was waiting for him next to the almond tree. The fuzzy husks of almond fruit lay rotting on the clay dirt, and their smell of bitter roses filled the air. She had shorn her hair into a brown helmet with a slight gold sheen. She moved to the doorway, and barred his entrance, her hand closed in a fist over her heart, her eyes staring past him. She was wearing a loose white shift. She didn't say anything. Instead, she opened her hand and held it out. The little gold baby shoe charm sparkled on her palm. Chico had bought it when Hilesca was born and put it on a gold chain around the baby's neck.

He took the charm, and Aurora turned her back to him, opened the door of the shack and closed it softly behind her. He breathed in the smell of bitter roses.

His clothes were in San Juan, and now he realized there wasn't much in the shack that he still had any claim to. Except her.

He knocked. "*Mi amor . . .* "

Silence. Like there was nobody inside. He stood on the dirt path at the front door of the shack for a while, letting music play in his head. Took a piss against the almond tree and looked at his watch. Forty minutes had passed. He went back to the door and called out again.

"The silence inside the shack was terrible, Fina. She wouldn't talk to me. I couldn't even hear her moving around. It was like she wasn't there. Like she had walked out the back door. But the shack didn't have one."

After that, Aurora never spoke to him again.

That silence that marked the end of one phase in his life crept inside of him. "It was like somebody turned a light or something on in my brain, and I had to see myself, but there wasn't a soundtrack like I was used to."

He went back to San Juan, but when the AMA bus drew up to the entrance at Llorens, he saw a parked sedan with tinted windows. He thought these might be Ferrera's famous thugs and decided not to get off the bus.

"I kept moving around, but you can't put off destiny. Ferrera's thugs weren't no myth. They picked me up at a *piragua* stand in the old city. They took me to the Playa del Perro at night, broke my ribs. They were about to shoot me when I ran and threw myself into the water. And I don't know how the hell I survived, really. A fisherman picked me up. He was one of those squatters in shacks on stilts under the Dos Hermanos bridge. There was a *curandero* there who healed me with poultices and shit."

One of his new squatter friends got him a fake ID, and he moved to New York, where he got gigs right away.

The silence faded for the most part.

"I knew she was dead, but once in a while I had this real strong sense that maybe she was alive somewhere. If not my baby girl herself, then her energy. Alive somewhere in the world, in something, in someone else."

Whenever I saw the girl near Chico, she was always being, well, so physical. Always accidentally bumping her melons up against him, taking the slightest opportunity to reach across him for the salt, sitting right up next to him on the bus stop bench. And she couldn't tell a story without putting her hands on his thigh, his neck, his face. Poor old Chico, trying to flick off those caresses like harmless insects while trying to get her to spill the beans. Or for all I knew, maybe after spilling his beans into her night after night.

The Friday of the first week after she arrived, I felt called upon to do just a little *fufú*: I put Hilesca's name on paper in a dish, smeared it with a potent mixture of gunpowder, monkey shit and that stinky grease *brujos* call "hate oil." I put the dish outside the back door downstairs, where I had seen the heifer copping smokes unbeknownst to Chico, or so I thought.

Another week passed, but homegirl didn't budge. I was beginning to think that Chico didn't mind having a minor sit on his lap, or push her titties under his nose. I thought that the inevitable would happen, but the strange thing is that nothing really happened beyond all that rubbing and touching. Or so Chico told me one morning.

I had heard his cases bumping along the stairway, so I arranged my extensions, opened the door and sort of pranced up to him doing one of my irresistible "hellowhatupthere" routines.

I turned and went back inside, hoping he'd follow. He stepped inside, but wouldn't sit down.

"This kid!" He flicked at his nose with a finger. "Weird shit."

He'd had a lot of sets at the Copa and the Latin Bistro in the last few weeks. They all started late and ended late, and he came home bone tired. He would stumble into his bedroom, pull off his clothes and throw himself naked on the bed and fall asleep like that.

He didn't know how long the girl who called herself Hilesca had been watching him, but one night he woke up, his eyes still half-closed, and saw her. She stood there for such a long time that he fell into a dream he had forgotten. He saw the zinc-roofed house in Puerto Rico where he had lived with Aurora. Aurora turned her back on him, went into the house and closed the door behind her. He kept on knocking on the door. Then the silence was such that he realized Aurora wasn't in the house anymore. The silence penetrated him. He opened his mouth to speak, but the words wouldn't come.

He opened his eyes and saw the girl still staring at him, her eyes shadowy sockets, her own silence like the silence in his dream.

From then on, he knew she was coming into his bedroom almost every night because he lay awake until she did. Sometimes he had an erection, especially if he'd done a few lines of *perico*. Sometimes he got it while she was there. And sometimes he was so tired, he fell asleep right away. Of course, there was a progression. One night she walked in, watched him for a while and just as he was falling asleep, she lay down on the bed next to him. He could smell the cheap drugstore perfume on her, and worse, he could feel the heat of those parts of her body that rose like bread through her shorts and tight T-shirt.

That silence from so long ago ballooned inside of him, to the extent that he felt he had left his real self behind at the club. His body was on its own, his *pinga* standing up like a toy soldier so that he had to pretend to flip over in his sleep. His attempt to control his body must have annoyed her because she leapt off the bed and stood there for what seemed like half an hour. He didn't turn his head or widen his eyes because that would have given away the game. He was afraid that she would touch him.

He paused, and looked down at my scuffed up hardwood floor. "But I wanted it, too."

"You wanted it?"

"Sure. Let's be honest. I wanted it. But I didn't act on it. There's a difference, you know."

Why the fuck did he want it? Unfortunately for me, the only way to ask this question was by knockout, so I grunted instead.

"I gotta go," he said suddenly. "I'm waiting on a call. There's a producer who wants to do my first song." A rare smile lit up his normally distracted features. He chuckled. "Well, really, my only song so far."

"Good luck." I only said it grudgingly because I didn't want him to go.

Chico came by the next morning wearing a purple short-sleeved shirt, and beige linen pants with gold flecks in the cloth. He hugged me, and gave me a kiss on one cheek, then the other. Even after we sat down at my kitchen table, I could still feel the wetness on my face.

"The studio wants to hear different versions of the song. They want me to line up different types of singers for it."

"Wow!"

He drank down the hot coffee like water. "And you aren't going to believe what else happened last night."

Sure enough, the girl had come to him. This time, she wasn't wearing any clothes.

Through his half-closed eyes he saw her naked for the first time. Not only could she not be his daughter, he didn't think she could be his ex-sister-in-law's kid either. Jahaira, his ex-wife's sister, was a woman with such intensely blue-black skin, sometimes it was hard to see her at night.

Hair hung from under Hilesca's arms and over her sex, tangled like Spanish moss, dark against the skin of a body that glowed white like those starry ceilings parents put up in kids' rooms.

That was the last time this grown Hilesca came into Chico's room, and he became completely still and quiet. His *pinga* saluted her as if it belonged to someone else. He watched her watch him. Casually, she poked a finger into her luxuriant bush.

He'd kept his eyes narrowed all those times, only open enough to catch important movements but not enough for it to be obvious he was awake.

His eyes opened wide now and he stared right at her. One of them couldn't stand the charade any longer. She stalked over to the bed and batted his erect penis.

Chico, brain fuzzy with pain and surprise, rocked back and forth, holding himself there until the stinging ebbed.

Then he sat up straight against the wall and yelled at her. "What are you doing?" He hadn't expected such an artless betrayal of the little ritual they'd set up.

The girl stood there with eyes like onyx. There was a thick silence. They just stared at each other, her nipples like lighthouses on the dunes of her chest, and his *pinga* like a chastised puppy.

"I have a question," she said.

"Naked? You swat me and then want to ask me questions when I'm naked and trying to recover?"

"I didn't want you to say no."

Then like an afterthought, she said, "Papi." The thin straight hair, so much not the hair of anyone that could have been his daughter, slid over her face like a curtain.

"I want to sing. I can sing, Papi. I want to be your lead singer."

He got up from the bed, grabbed her by the shoulders and shook that pale hairy Betty Boop until she pushed him away, her breasts brushing against his arm, like soft little pillows he wanted to punch.

She pointed at the moss at her crotch and then bounced a hand off her breasts. "I'll call the cops on you, Papi. I'll go to the door naked and let them come to their own conclusions. They'll take you away for bothering me."

"You little bitch!"

"You bothering me now, yeah?"

He had fantasized about simply watching her play him, letting her take it as far as she could, to see if at some point something changed between them. Maybe that was as much intimacy as he could take.

He said through his teeth, "I'd have to tell them I'm not your papi. My only daughter died when she was just a baby."

The girl got quiet and even paler, like something squirming under a rock or in a cave, and he was thinking maybe she was the dead Hilesca come for him, Hilesca all grown up in death, and white from death, come to ask him why he hadn't paid for her hospital bills.

Her silence reminded him of Aurora. His ex could get quiet like that when she was angry, like she did when he'd shown up for the last time at their zinc-roofed house out on the island. She handed him the gold charm, then turned her back on him, quiet as if her rage was a cherished secret.

"What do you have to say for yourself?"

There was a pause, as if she was considering her response.

Homeboy hated himself at that moment for begging for a reaction from her. Who the hell was she to be mad at him because he'd called her bluff? But it was true, her gestures, her silence, reminded him of Aurora.

Finally, she turned around and said, "So why did you go along with it then? You let me call you 'Papi.' You told the *bruja* downstairs I was your daughter. What's up with that?"

"I want to know why you're pretending to be my daughter."

The girl's eyes looked like black rubber balls. "'Cause I want to find out about my mami and my papi. Titi Jahaira said you probably were my papi. Plus, I saw you in the papers. Before that, I didn't know you were such hot shit. And you know what? I can sing."

Chico laughed. "You and every other Puerto Rican." He grabbed the crumpled sheet and covered his whole body with it, from chest to legs. "How do you know Jahaira?"

"I told you. She's my aunt. She took me when I was a baby. We came to New York. She raised me."

The girl put her arm over her breasts and with her other hand plucked at the bottom sheet on Chico's bed so that homeboy had to move his ass. She wrapped the sheet around her body. "My mami left. Or maybe she died. Nobody knows. She named me Hilesca, but she called me Alba. Alba Hilesca, to remind her of her first kid. That's what Titi Jahaira said."

Aurora, the mother he thought she was lying about, was a shade or two darker than Chico himself, the color of wet sand in the setting sun, a woman with no hair anywhere on her body except the soft gold kinked storm cloud on her head.

"I don't know if you're Aurora's second daughter. What I do know is that you sure as hell ain't nothing of mine. Tomorrow, you better clear out."

"Please, Chico man, just let me sing for you first!"

"You gotta be kidding."

But she started singing "*Noche de ronda*." That's a song that most Latinos love—those with a foot here and a foot back there, I mean. He let her finish it.

As it turned out, Hilesca, whose name was really Alba Sánchez, courtesy of Coop City, the Bronx, could belt out songs ranging from squeaky *merengues* to the best classic salsa. But what she could sing most soulfully were jazz ballads.

And Chico ended up liking the way Alba sang the song the record company wanted to produce. It was a song he had been working on for a long time, a song about the love that one day decides it can't love you back, the migrating love that doesn't stay the same, the love that might come back. Some shape, some form, some day.

But now love migrates; hey, hey, love migrates.

He said that if she really was Aurora's daughter, he couldn't send her packing just yet. I couldn't help but think he was attracted to the girl because she reminded him of his first love.

Love migrates so that new love can come your way.

THREE
THE *PALERO*

That goddamn Lolita was still squatting in Chico's living room. Homeboy would diss the kid for her lying ways, but then he'd rave about how perfect her voice was, how she was like some sort of female version of Marc Anthony or even —sacrilege!—Hector Lavoe. He was going to take her to try-outs at Cleopatra's Needle.

So I decided to up the ante and go see Tata Victor Tumba Fuego, Master of Fire. Unlike me, he had all the power that comes from faith and fear. He was my badass Godfather in the magic arts.

Thugs in do-rags sat on the steps outside Victor's building near 106th and Lexington. A middle-aged guy in a suit with dandruff specks on the shoulders stood talking to them. When they saw me, one of the thugs pocketed something, stopped talking and just stared into space until the suit guy took a hint and left.

Metal framed the building's glass door. Stained and cracked yellow tiles paved the lobby floor.

Tata Victor usually left the cracker jacks box door open, so I pushed at it with my hip. The paper grocery bag I was carrying jumped, and I almost dropped it. A vapor of feathers and shit wafted up to me. Inside the bag was a rooster I'd picked up at the East River livestock market, legs and beak bound. I let the main door close behind me, turned and knocked on the door of the reading room.

"Come in." If a bull could speak, it would have Tata Victor's gravelly voice.

I opened the door. I breathed in a top note of earth and leaves. Under that my nostrils were tickled by the sweet scent of old blood and high-proof rum mixed with the dirt in Victor's cauldrons.

Victor sat behind a plain wooden table, giving the impression of a big tall tree, an ancient Ceiba. He had lately lost a lot of weight, so his clothes kind of hung on him. Most *paleros* and *santeros* are built like houses, and Victor used to be, too. Then his wife left him for a Miami *santero*, and he stopped eating like he used to. On some level it seemed like he wanted to shrink. But no matter how much a six-foot-four guy slouches, it ain't going to make him shrink.

A goat's head had been thrust on a wooden stake in the largest cauldron. The goat's eyes were glazed open, and the animal's black hair was spiky, probably with honey. A recent sacrifice. I thought I saw a tear floating in one of its eyes, and I looked away.

There were twelve iron cauldrons of varying sizes, all planted with peeled tree branches, or *palos*, and adorned with all kinds of stuff: dolls with glass eyes and shorn hair, handcuffs, stuffed animals, toy cars and trains, animal skulls and more.

The largest cauldron, the one with the goat's head, housed Zarabanda, warrior *nkisi*. Two blackened, rusty machetes were stuck in the middle of the pot, and the winding horns of three rams encased the *palos* sticking out of it. Zarabanda was such a fierce warrior that an iron chain was wrapped around the pot to keep his power in place until needed.

"When are you doing your cutting?" Victor fixed his eyes, brown with burgundy lights, on me.

"I'm waiting until I get all the money together."

I was bullshitting him, and he knew it. His eyes flicked a little. "It's just a few cuts on your thumbs and back."

"I know."

Trouble was there was no coming back from the cutting. To be cut in *Palo* meant that you might see all the *nfuiris*, all the spirits of the dead and all the *nkisis*, the gods of the woods and wind and even the few born lately into the street. You might see them better than any human could. Many a *palero* had been driven mad by the dead seen constantly awake or in dreams.

But more important, once you were cut, all the *nkisis* and *nfuiris* saw you. You were now part of their world and could never get away from them. It was like TV monitors from the world of the dead watching you 24/7, and that idea scared the shit out of me.

The cowries were on the table in front of Victor, and he was getting ready to throw them.

"Right now, I just want to do a simple *consulta*."

"No *consulta* is simple." I had to look in his eyes again. "What do you really want?" he asked.

"There's a guy."

"The bus driver."

I frowned.

He smiled. "Somebody else."

"There's this chick who's distracting him. I got hair and other shit from both of them."

"Hold on." Victor put up a hand and then threw the cowry shells, still grinning. Three cowries landed with their little serrated mouths up and two down.

"Hah!" said Victor. "The Ancient One speaks."

Victor had inherited the Ancient One from his father, and his father from his grandfather, going all the way back to Africa.

The Ancient One's pot was now almost as big as Zarabanda's, and I looked at it. The center, the secret, could not be seen because there were so many long, splintered, pieces of wood, sticking out of the pot, a few of them shot through with nails. There was a bull horn, too, a black stick wrapped with pieces of old black cloth, and a black hat that still had the remains of old-ass ancient gold thread sticking out of it.

I suppressed a shiver. Unlike Zarabanda, who was a pantheon *nkisi*, a god really, the Ancient One was one of the *nfuiris*, and the oldest of all the dead that worked for Victor.

Victor looked up. The Victor who looked up seemed like the same man, same thousand-year-old look in the eyes, same ironic yet kind curl to the lips, but now he was also addressing the Ancient One.

And there was silence as Victor's eyes kinda rolled in his head, and he took on that white-eyed look of the possessed in B-movies.

"The Ancient One says all is not what it seems."

Victor stood up, rocked like an ocean liner against the table until he was next to me. He pulled me by the hand over to where the pot sat next to the window.

He fit one of his hands into the thicket of *palos*, and then with the other, he pulled the clump apart.

Victor grunted. "Take it!"

"What?"

"Take it, he wants you to take it."

I put out a hand and touched something warm; I pulled it back quick.

"Hold him in the place between the eye sockets, go ahead."

I pulled the warm thing up. It was light, a gray crumbled skull, laced all over in green fungus, the sockets crusted with dirt.

I tried to give it back to Victor.

"No, hold him in the palm of your hand."

It seemed to me that it was . . . smiling. "It's burning my fingers!"

"He has something to say to you."

Victor started to speak to the skull in fragments of the Congo language that had been passed down from Africa to the islands and then to Spanish Harlem. I knew some words like "*nganga*," "*mpungo*," "*bakisi*" or "*kimpungulu*." I did and didn't know what he was saying. I sort of knew he was pleading and urging. He was coaxing the skull.

I saw the skull's smile deepen. And then I felt the warmth, a pulsing in my hand. Its jaws started working up and down. And then it got mad hot, but there was no way I would let it go now. I wanted to hear what it had to say.

Victor stopped muttering in Congo language, and said, "He says that if you want what isn't yours, you owe a sacrifice. Will you give that sacrifice?"

I nodded.

Now I heard muffled sounds in the air. Words that sounded like they were coming from behind a wall and yet coming closer. They weren't Victor's words, but they didn't seem to be coming from the skull in my hand either. It was like they were being pulled out of the air itself.

There was a connection between the words building in the air and the heat in the skull, which was making the sweat drop off my hands. The words were pushing themselves into existence as through a thick, otherworldly boundary. The air itself was filled with a kind of soundless panting.

"Wooo . . . " I felt full, horribly full, and my stomach seemed like it was going to come apart.

I started to panic. "What . . . what . . . ?" I was sweating all over. I could smell the stink in my armpits, the fishiness of my cunt.

My mouth opened, even though I didn't want it to. A voice came from me, but it wasn't my voice.

"Wo-man, wo-man . . . " The deep sound welled up from my stomach, but the more it welled, the fuller I felt. "Woman can be driven away, but first, first she must come. She will come and then be driven away."

The voice stopped. I doubled over retching, and then like vomit it came again.

"The dog . . . was hung on the . . . the mango tree. Zarabanda's dog."

The dog? I tried to speak back to it . . . because then I remembered the mango tree.

A dog strung up on a mango tree, the leaves from the mango glistening from the wet of a night storm.

"Fill the *bóveda* glasses with water."

And then the other voice disappeared, and I was speaking, me, Fina, in a hoarse voice. "Fill the glasses in my *bóveda* . . . for a dog?"

My *bóveda* was made up of nine small glasses filled with water that Victor had told me to keep for the *nkisis* and for all of my dead, even the ones I didn't know. I had it on the mantelpiece in my apartment.

Victor took the skull away. My hands were cold. Victor was now holding the skull, and I could see by the way he held it that it was still hot. The jaw was still working up and down, and it continued to speak, in those unbearable, muffled sounds, telling Victor secrets I could no longer hear.

Victor nodded, as he listened, and when the jaw stopped its chewing movement, he sat silent, his eyes closed.

I breathed out, glad that the skull had stopped speaking, and that its voice wasn't pushing out of me any more like some Evil Dead baby.

But its jaws were still moving up and down.

Victor chuckled. "We have to feed him."

Animal blood is the offering favored by the *nkisis* and *nfuiris*. And I understand the primitive principle behind it all. Blood is the most sacred form of energy, and when the spirits drink they become enlivened to help us in this world. But shit, we ain't on the island no more, we don't sacrifice in the mountains of Africa or Cuba; we do it in our apartments. Can't we substitute and modernize a little with the other aspects of the religion? Streamline and make it more up to date?

While the skull was speaking, the rooster had only rustled now and then in its bag. But when I pulled it out of the bag it squawked and sprayed shit on my hands.

Victor took a knife from where it lay next to little glass bottles filled with oils and powders. He put the knife in my hand. "You do it."

"Oh no, no. You know I've never done it."

"It's time to start. You want this so bad, you need to do it yourself."

I bit my lip. Standing behind me, he helped me take the rooster by its ropy legs, so much like plant stalks from another world. It flapped and squawked; the poor sucker knew what was coming.

I aimed for the center of the bird's neck. I'd seen this done enough times. The animal gave one last baby wail before the knife thunked its neck, baring bone. A terrible hot smell of chicken feathers, blood and shit filled the air.

"The bird dies so you can live. Act like you feel its death," said Victor. "Feel that it dies so you can keep on living and loving."

In the end, the rooster broke into a death rattle that shook its whole body, and I lost hold of it again. Victor severed its head, which fell onto the reading table. An eye like a bead stared right up at me.

Victor was looking at me with a little bit of pity. "This is child's play. Guess what happens when you cut a ram's throat in a room this size?"

I wasn't going to tell him this, but fucking wild horses were never going to drag me to kill a ram or a goat, no matter what. Just the idea of it made me want to pass the fuck out.

"Stop making faces like a little girl and give me the things that belong to the lovers."

I took out combings of long black hair and the pieces of a red shirt that Chico had thrown out. I'd found both the hair and cloth in the garbage dumpsters in our basement. I laid them on the newspaper-covered table.

Victor poured some of the dying animal's blood from its neck onto the tissue and shirt pieces. He placed the skull on a dish and poured the rest of the blood on top of it.

The skull glistened with blood, and the skull's half-broken jaw slowed, then finally stopped, chewing.

In an empty pot in his kitchen, Victor set a blob of crude
brown wax, on which he sprinkled drops of a black substance
from a tiny glass vial. He turned on a gas burner, put the pot
on it and took an iron spoon from one of the kitchen drawers
and stirred the oil into the wax. Then he poured the wax mixture into a metal bowl that held the bloodied shirt remnants.
In another metal bowl, he added the hair and some lipstick-
stained pieces of tissue that I had seen Alba throw into a trash
can in front of the building.

I drank a glass of water while we waited for the wax to cool.

And then I remembered. The tree stood on the dirt path in
front of the shack. A tall old mango tree, the leaves shiny and
dark on top and pale green underneath. No fruit. The dog, a
bony black mutt, had been hung on a rope on one of the thick-
er branches.

I had forgotten the dog. It was my Abuela who showed me.
She grabbed me by the scruff of my T-shirt and dragged me.
The T-shirt actually tore, but I followed her.

I looked up at the tree. The dog's swollen tongue hung out
of its mouth.

"Why?" I asked her.

"Your father is a *brujo!*" Abuela worshipped only Jesus and
the Virgin Mary. "Your father strung the animal up. He wor-
ships the devil, him and that woman of his."

And later, days later, maybe weeks, I walked by the river
with my father. He told me to find the *morivivi*, the sensitive
plant that closes its leaves when it's touched.

I bent down and touched the purplish feathery leaf. The
tiny filaments slowly furled shut.

I asked my father if he was a devil-worshipper.

His face drew into shadows. All I could remember were
those fierce eyes.

"Do you think I worship the devil?"

I shook my head. I was a little kid. "Spirits in water?"

He nodded. "*Nkisis*, Fina, in water, in trees, everywhere, even in the air we breathe."

"And the dog?" I pressed. "Who killed it? What does it mean?"

"Fill the *bóveda* glasses with water for me, *nena*. Promise to remember me when I am gone."

And it wasn't long after that one night that I woke to the terrible sound of a firing squad, the sound of voices crying out, of people crying out as they were shot to death. It was rain on the zinc roof. A hurricane.

My father was there watching me. "Got to sleep, *nena*. It's a storm. Nothing to worry about."

Over his shoulder a familiar face: dark skin, brown eyes and strangely bright red hair. His girlfriend Caterina. Her mouth smiled, but not her eyes.

In the morning, he was gone, and so was Caterina.

"That *diablo* ran off with his *diabla* woman," said my grandmother.

I had a fever that night. And afterward I forgot about the dog hanging from the mango tree.

Victor told me to make male and female dolls. I sculpted crude figures like maybe a kid would, breasts and a big ass, a man doll with a penis sticking straight out.

I brought a hand up to my nose. It smelled of camphor, and something stale, an old-lady type of smell.

We stood outside the door of the reading room.

"When the wax dries I'll put those dolls in the reading room. And every day I'll push them away from each other under the eyes of the *nkisis* and the dead. They will gain shade. They will grow apart. They will lose each other among the *kiyumbas*."

I was thrilled by that. Adam and Eve in the cosmos of the reading room. And I touched my stomach on the spot where that other voiced had bloomed.

On my way out of Victor's building, I almost stepped on a girl thug on the steps. A girl thug, but she wasn't wearing a do-rag.

"Hey, *bruja*, how you doing?"

I looked down incredulously at a pair of melted black wax eyes. She was wearing a long-sleeved white Lycra shirt, Nikes and tight jeans.

Words, the words that can sometimes be as strong as *fufús*, and those that can just be real good weapons, they failed me.

"Hah hah." She sort of stuck her tongue out at me. Or maybe she was licking her tiny red lips. "You ain't the only one that goes to Tumba Fuego for help. I'm-a waiting for my appointment."

I finally got my wits back. "Who the fuck are you, after all?"

She stood up, and I saw that as usual she didn't have a bra on and as usual she was pushing out her tits for maximum exposure.

"Me?" She lightly ran a hand over her boobs. "I'm just a girl from somewhere, and that's nowhere, Doña Fina. I got no father, no mother, no roots. But I got talent. I want something."

She sucked in her whole tiny mouth and looked at me with eyes that blazed but seemed kind of dead at the same time. "Don't you want something?"

A thought almost took my breath away. *But first she must come.* Damn if this wasn't the most efficient *fufú* ever!

And I nodded, and said yes, yes, I did.

FOUR
MISS UNIVERSE'S PANTIES

To make up for the fact that Gus wasn't paying the rent no more, I started working as a secretary at The Balder School. Yeah, it ain't my calling, but I can do secretary in a pinch. I went to typing school and can type eighty words a minute. I may be a plus size, but I've got nimble fingers and I like words on a page. I read a lot of shit, from *The Times* to Victorian poems to urban trash novels. Words on the page can be like *fufús* unto themselves.

The building I was supposed to work in was a brownstone neo-something-or-other on the Upper East Side on 90th St. I walked in and did a double-take when I saw the place didn't have no security guard or metal detectors at the door. I saw a tall blonde boy in the school's uniform of gray pants and a white shirt walk up the stairs to the second floor. Aside from that, the place was real quiet and gray, like a bad painting of an interior space, and like no school I'd ever been to before.

Looking spiffy in my chosen camouflage—a long black skirt and a white button down shirt—I went into the office belonging to my new boss, the Headmaster, Hiram Beltoff.

Between the floor-to-ceiling windows and a huge desk carved from different types and colors of inlaid wood sat a soft-bodied, bald man in his mid-fifties with a big bushy red-haired moustache. There was a big state-of-the-art desktop computer on one end of the desk and four piles of neatly stacked papers on the other end.

He looked up. "Can I help you?" High twang. A suit that looked like textured silk. An old queen from the "Remember the Alamo" South.

"I'm the new secretary."

"Oh." He looked at me head to toe, but kind of out the sides of his eyes. "Josephine Meta?"

"Ho-se-fin-ah Ma-ta."

He kept darting glances at my hair. The extensions were tied up so that they flowed down my back, but if I turned my head sharp up or down, they made a chica-chica-chic sound. I think it pissed off old Beltoff. I wanted to let rip a laugh, but I can do a stone face when I need to, and I did.

"Ha-rem Bail-toff to you," he said, not meeting my eye. "Well, Josefeena, as long as you can write and type adequately and do basic errands, we should have no problem."

Adequately? Basic errands? What was this condescending shit? "I'll try my best to do my best," I said. Or some shit like that.

He quickly restacked the four piles of paper on his desk. Then he pointed behind him somewhere. "Your office is there," he said.

On the far right there was a door next to the big windows. I strode over, opened it. The room was a windowless cubbyhole with a vomit-colored rug and a desktop computer about seventy-five percent smaller than Beltoff's.

I went back to his big office. "No printer?"

"You'll share the printer with the other staff in this suite. I have an office manager, an accounts manager and there are two other secretaries. A Headmaster needs a respectable staff. Each secretary has specific duties."

I discovered on my second day that my specific duties for the time being seemed to be typing letters firing people's asses. Beltoff dictated eleven letters to me that day—all letters letting faculty and staff know their contracts had not been renewed.

When I was done typing, he looked at the first printouts and complained about the typos.

I looked at the typos. "Two typos in eleven letters is pretty good." I shrugged. What a petty little twerp! I didn't think an Ivy League secretary could do much better. It occurred to me that he probably liked to terrorize the types that ended up working the secretary routine. Well, in the end, condescension or no condescension, his caterpillar body told me I would have the final fucking punch. If it ever came down to that. Which it wouldn't. What the fuck could make it worth it?

"No typo is better."

"Goes without saying I'm correcting them." I went on with my fake honey routine. "You from Texas?"

"Kansas."

Texas was the Lone Star State, hot-assed cowboys and Mexican Americans coming into their own. Kansas . . .

"Wizard of Oz!" I bellowed.

He rolled his eyes, but didn't say nothing, and then looked shiftily away. He took up a letter that had no typos, put it in the already addressed envelope and passed one of those little sponge things with a handle over the gummed part. Then he sealed the envelope.

"I'm putting this in Ashley Duval's mailbox myself." His face was red, his eyes liquid with excitement.

He didn't like me, but my size made him leery. As for me, I thought he was a goddamn laughable ass, but I needed the job and I knew what the workaday world was like. Tata Victor's skulls and bones were a helluva a lot more alive than people who pushed paper for a living.

But to live sometimes you have to die a little.

At work, a few days later, I sat in my little windowless cubbyhole with the vomit-orange rug. It was so hot I kept the door open, typing and printing letters for Beltoff. Folding envelopes. At one point I looked up and there was a gray-haired woman with pink-framed glasses staring at me. She wore boring navy pumps, and a gray suit that fit her like clothes on a hanger.

"Is one of those letters for me?'

"Who're you?'

"Lori Shellman. I teach Psychology and History of Science."

"Oh." I knew who she was. She had filed some sort of complaint against Beltoff. "No."

She let out a little breath of relief, but her blue eyes were still faded from worry, so I said, "I don't think you're going to get one of these. You made that badass complaint, and now he's too afraid that if he gets rid of you, it'll look like retaliation."

Her blue eyes lit up like the sparks they were meant to be.

I can't say I felt any regrets when Alba, or whatever her name was, came by to bitch and moan a few days later.

She stood in my doorway with her hair hanging greasily over her face. For once she wasn't channeling Betty Boop or Jessica Rabbit. Instead she wore baggy pants and a loose T-shirt and one of them baseball hats with the batter on it.

"Chico's kicking me out." Alba looked down so I couldn't see her eyes under the baseball cap, but her voice was all trembly. "You happy now?"

"You mean your 'father,' right?" I put on a stone face. I didn't invite her in, but I wanted to enjoy the moment.

"I thought maybe he was." She looked away. "Anyway, my Titi Jahaira went back to PR. I need a place to stay."

"If I think of something, I'll let you know."

"You don't get it!" The kid actually stamped her foot. "I can't stay there tonight. Miss Universe's panties are hanging in the bathroom."

My stone face fell off, and she looked up. She had shadows under her eyes, but now there was a wicked upturn to her smile. "Didn't you know about Miss Universe?"

"Yeah sure, but that was . . . back on the island." I cleared my throat. "Wasn't it?"

"She's here. She's splitting up with her husband, and she got Chico eating out of her hand."

The girl talked nonstop, but after she told me there was some new (or old?) lover shacked up there with Chico, I didn't hear much else. I felt lightheaded. Damn, what was up with this *fufú*? Now the girl was on the outs, but apparently there was somebody new slithering up and down the stairs. Somebody else I hadn't even seen.

But first she must come.

A vague threat caught me: " . . . and if I can't find nothing by tonight, I'm crashing with you, *bruja*."

I heard the building door clunk shut, and I didn't have any shame about bounding up the stairs two at a time.

I knocked on his door. Quiet. Was it the quiet of somebody listening behind the door? I knocked again, but with my strong hand this time and real hard. And then, I tried the handle.

The door opened. It didn't even occur to me not to enter.

"Chico," I called, uncertainly. I said, "Hey!" Then I yelled louder. There was no response. I pulled the door shut behind me, locked it and I went to the bathroom.

Just a typical New York City undersized bathroom with a cracked tile floor and one of them windows closed tight on a back alley filled with dumpsters.

The so-called panties were a little lace strip as red as a lollipop and about as big. I stared at it. Something like that would just sink into my ass.

And then I went to the bedroom. Chico's tongue-pink shirt was hanging on the back of a chair. On his dresser: a black bow tie and a bottle—Hermès Orange Vert. A small painted wooden statue of Santa Bárbara in her red robes standing next to her tower. Little silver *coquí* frog cufflinks. Only a Puerto Rican could like those.

Chanel lipstick, Michael Kors perfume. Not stuff the girl would use. I opened the lipstick and put some on. It was fragrant and had a grainy texture. *Red Dream*.

The bed was covered in a thick quilt made of orange, yellow, purple silk pieces; flowered blue and plaid cotton patches; even tiny mirrors and beads. I sat on the quilt and fingered a little mirror. My heart was hammering. I thought I might find something really important, something secret that would reveal Chico to me.

I tried to take in the atmosphere. There was that faintly bloody smell of rum in the room, and maybe Chinese food. And that underlying odor of wood baking in the summer of a New York City apartment.

I looked in the closet. It was a pretty wide closet. There were pants folded and hanging, and all those colored silk shirts. There were maybe three pairs of men's shoes, and a few cardboard boxes.

If I crouched near a box, I might not be seen in the dark if someone was just reaching in.

There was a dress, a flowered green and white dress. The fabric was soft and plush between my fingers. Escada, 100% silk. Size 4. Even I might not look bad in a dress like that, ten sizes bigger, of course.

Was that all? Was that the secret? A new woman who dressed in clothes that maybe cost what I paid for a month of rent.

I had a floaty feeling. I was close, wasn't I?

I opened the first drawer of a little night table. It was filled with a mess of documents. I saw the blue of a passport. I lifted a yellowed document: *Acta de nacimiento*: Vega Baja, Chico de León. . . .

I passed a hand under the lumpy futon and the rickety frame on one side of the bed, and then the other.

There were some pictures, the kind we used to take in our Ancient History and get drugstore developed. Old sepia colored pictures, a little faded. People from jaundiced white to milk chocolate posed for their pictures under palm trees, next to a car, next to pigs and goats, next to a river, next to the ocean, next to a sandbar joining the river and the ocean.

I stopped and examined that one. A woman stood at the juncture of glassy ocean water and dark muddy river and its sandy shore. She had long wild kinked hair with gold highlights here and there. She was a small woman with a big bust and big hips, yellowish skin. Wasn't Aurora darker? This woman had a beautiful face, though: a heart-shaped face with eyes that kind of mocked you, but in a good way.

I heard a key jiggling in the apartment door.

My heart beat faster, and then I couldn't feel it at all, and I took a fumbling dive into the deep closet.

I left the door a little bit ajar. Not because I found it that way.

Because you know, I ain't stupid. I talk stupid sometimes because you can make a point better when people aren't expecting much from you. And what I'm trying to say is that from the moment I entered homeboy's crib, I had to decide what I'd do if he came home, whether it was even worth being caught. But that closet was deep. And a part of me almost wanted to be caught.

I crouched down, because it made me feel like I was out of sight, but let's face it: it's impossible for somebody my size to really hide, even in a deep closet.

She was talking to him in that sort of nasal accent typical of island Puerto Ricans—but it sounds good in women's voices. Airy, but commanding. *"Ay, querido. ¿Tú sabes? Ay sí, tú sabes cómo fue. Eso es así. Qué bueno que todo esto te haya salido tan bien."*

And then some heavily accented English. "She wanted him, *mi amor*, because you were with me."

There was a strange tone in his voice. "I don't think she wanted him. How could she? Why would she?"

"But you want me."

And then a silence, a giggle, the muffled torture of the futon frame. More giggling.

"Look at it, do you like the way it looks?"

"It looks like real high-class cunt."

She giggled. "High class? *¿Por qué?*"

"It's blushing because it's wet. It's like the inside of an orchid."

He made a growling jokey sound. Then there was silence. I imagined that he was biting deep into the orchid, deep into the orchid opening up for him, its pistil stiffening and growing ever more beautiful, and I closed my eyes and pressed my hand against my groin.

I was lucky that after a long time, after they had cried out, and laughed, and after the little necklace of pearls came undone inside of me too, I heard him snoring.

So I carefully unstuck myself from the box my ass had smashed down, and I pushed open the door.

I tried to steal away stealthily. But maybe "stealthy" is just an idea I got from urban novels and whatnot.

Maybe it was finally my fat breath that gave me away. When I was tiptoeing ridiculously into the living room, I felt a god-damn push.

I turned.

I couldn't see her face clearly in the dark. She had put on some sort of long red negligee. But in the heat I could still smell the sweat and body fluids on her. She smelled like ham and vanilla.

"Who are you?" Whispery for some reason. And because she didn't start screaming right away, I didn't bolt right away either.

She was tall, that much I could see, and through the silky negligee I saw nipples as spiky as cloves.

Then she must come.

In hindsight, I must have said this to piss her off in advance of knowing her: "I'm . . . Aurora."

"*¿Qué?*" She retreated, brought her hands up to her face. "*Ay ¿qué? Ay no,*" or something like that. Then she sat down on the floor, and started to rock back and forth starting what an Irish witch I met once at a Wiccan conference called "sublime keening," a sound like a low-volume modified scream that flowed with the rhythm of her rocking.

Then Dazed and Confused woke up in the bedroom. "Baby?" A high panicky note.

I rushed to the door, undid the lock and bolted down the stairs.

In my apartment, I sat at my table, expecting them to come and knock down my door, and drag me to the police station, but a good hour and a half passed, and all I did was think about him doing to me what he had done to her.

Would he like my orchid, vulgar thing that it was, big and bulbous and overgrown, a different species altogether than any pretty little wild little island thing?

FIVE
EXTREME MAKEOVER

In the light of day, though, it seemed almost like it hadn't happened.

I was coming up the front steps, they were coming down, or maybe vice versa. Or maybe he knocked on my door and said "Hey, Fina, last week it was jailbait, this week it's Miss Universe." Shit, I don't know how I ran into them, but I had been thinking of this whole Miss Universe thing and wondering which one it was because that tiny island has produced six of them at least, including Marc Anthony's ex.

So many because we PRs, we be hot. That's what we hype anyway.

And . . . it was Isis Sandín.

"I saw you on TV when you won the contest!" I bellowed. "You look the same."

No lie. The chick's face didn't look any older than when she'd won Miss Universe fifteen years ago. Green eyes, perfect little model's nose, pulpy lips with just a little touch of gloss on them. There was maybe some age in her slightly wider waist and hips. And there was looseness in her arms. But hey, I have serious fat sliding around in my batwings.

When she recognized me, her face went through a kind of Jim Carrey routine. Even that on her didn't seem that ridiculous. But when she was back in her stride, she gave me the onceover. Then she stepped back like a street dog was charging her.

That pissed me off, even though I recognized she had a right to be startled, what with the weirdness last night.

You see, I was predisposed to hating this bitch's kind: light-skinned girls who went to Catholic school on the island and to finishing schools in the States. Girls who straightened their hair and dyed it blonde. That's not it, though. In that way they're not so different from their dark sisters. When I was a kid, I spent sleepless nights with hair wrapped around my head and pinned in a dooby.

Coming to New York in 1995 liberated me from all that crap. But all that straightening and dyeing made a chick like Isis into what girls like me could never be—white as a soap opera star. That was it. Born and bred to be a fat cat's wife in San Juan, shop at Plaza Las Américas, pick up the husband at the *Capitolio* in the Mercedes, go to mass on Sunday with a brood of moon-white *blanquito* babies, while the senator shacked up in a motel out on the island with a teenager from Barrio Adentro, Pa' Fuera or Del Otro Lado, a cheerful, calculating dark-skinned girl like me.

Just to mind game with her, I boomed "Isisita!" I threw all my glorious ghetto fat at her, my belligerent boobs and pumpernickel arms.

She gasped and shook free, trying really hard to stay gracious and distant, but unable to shake off GETTING FREAKED NOW.

Chico looked puzzled, then piped up, "Fina's the neighborhood *bruja*."

"You're a witch?" Now she was staring into my eyes, smiling carefully, trying to make good.

"Yeah."

"She's real good at it," said Chico.

The homegirl now had her contemplative look on. I know that look. It's the look that people get before they ask me to do a reading for them. To stall any asks, I said, "Did I tell you that Alba is crashing here for a few days?"

And then I either shut the door in their faces or ran up or down the stairs.

When I told Lori Shellman in a fleeting hallway conversation that I was known to some in my neighborhood as a witch, she responded, "Oh, so you read the cards!" I didn't bother correcting her idea that I was a tarot card reader. Education, as far as I'm concerned, happens through showing, not telling.

So when she invited me to have lunch with her in the faculty dining room, I was sure she was going to pay for my lunch and ask for a reading. What she wanted though was something that wasn't up my alley. Or maybe just not worth my while.

First she told me that Beltoff fired perfectly good teachers if he couldn't get along with them.

"Uh huh," I said, like that was news to me. I was the one typing up the letters. "You got lettuce in your teeth," I said helpfully.

She ran her tongue over her front teeth, but didn't dislodge the lettuce, and kept on talking. Since Beltoff had a hard time getting along with almost everybody, he was firing a lot of people and hiring flunkies that lived, worked and partied in his asshole.

"What else is new? Power corrupts. And absolute power, etc, etc." I joked.

She told me about Howells in History whom Beltoff had fired because Howells had voted against Beltoff when the latter had run for head of History a few years ago; Hernández in Spanish whom Beltoff demoted to substitute because Hernández had told other faculty that Beltoff's rival for headmaster was a better candidate; Abernathy in Philosophy, whom Beltoff denied some important teaching prize because Abernathy challenged Beltoff at assembly meetings; Smith in English. . . . The list seemed endless.

I didn't even bother asking her how she knew all these suppositions were true. But on the other hand, I didn't forget the bottled-up glee that made Beltoff's face so pink when he signed those letters.

"Yeah, he sucks," I shrugged. "What's it to me?"

She leaned in real close so I could smell the red onions from the Greek salad on her breath. "Here's your chance to do some good for people here," she whispered.

She wanted me to break into Beltoff's computer files and see if I could find dirt on him. A secret big or small. The faculty, or those that were left of the old guard, had been trying for years to file official complaints against him. Now they wanted to try the unofficial way.

"Look, Lori. I mean, Miss Shellman."

"You can call me Lori," she said. A little crease started to form between her eyebrows because she could tell I wasn't warming up to this project.

I smiled at her. "Lori." She was not a bad person. I could tell that just as well as I could tell that Beltoff was a major asshole. "I'm not crazy about the guy. I think it's terrible that he fires people who don't deserve it. But I'm just a secretary. There's not much I can do. He's my boss."

"But, Fina, aren't you a Doo-ha?"

"*Bruja.*"

"Yeah, yeah. I'm sorry. '*Broo—ha.*' As such, can't you come up with ways to . . . you know, get into the guy's head?"

"I ain't that kind of *bruja*. At least not yet. I do *fufús* mainly."

"Phew-phews?"

"Stress the second syllable. *Foo-FOO.*" If you want a man, you cover his picture in honey, perfumes and other sweet things. If you want to control somebody, you can put his picture in your shoe and step on it all the time."

"I love that, Fina! Oh, it's so symbolic, isn't it? Do these *foo-foos* work?"

I wasn't no Tata Victor. Presuming Victor wasn't doing magic tricks, I couldn't make a skull speak, I couldn't hypnotize Hiram Beltoff and I couldn't chant a spell to make his nasty files fly out of his computer and into mine.

"Sure my honey and monkey shit spells work most of the time, but that's because they take advantage of what you smart people call suggestion."

I moved my head close to her now, widening my eyes: "Sometimes my spells are unpredictable. They don't work, but they offer symbolic relief. They're metaphors for what you want reality to be. It's all therapy!"

She smiled at me.

I couldn't help liking the homegirl. She had that look of a beat-up workhorse that has one last mean and powerful kick left in it.

I shook my head. "They can be unpredictable sometimes. Yeah." That was it. What I needed to tell her. "They weren't really made for white people, or non-Latinos. And sometimes they can backfire on 'em."

It was three o'clock in the afternoon. Victor was still asleep. *Paleros* work all night and rest during the day, so it was still early for him. I was sitting on the plastic-covered couch in the living room, which was next to the reading room, watching "Extreme Makeover" with Victor's kid, Eugenio, or Genio for short.

Genio was an unusual kid. For example, there was a big bird perching on his shoulder staring now at me with its little onyx jewel of an eye, and now with a squawk at TV. It was really Genio who was watching "Extreme Makeover." I was just watching him watch it. He was bug-eyed in his concentration.

Genio was like Victor in some ways: in the eyes that glowed black with a demonic red shine in them, and the impassive demeanor that hinted that his slow-moving body could be roused very gradually to a great and powerful effort. But in other ways he must have taken after his mother. I never met her, but I heard she had run off with a Cuban *santero* from Miami. Genio was freckled, and had short, coarse, curly hair. Also, unlike Victor, who usually wore jeans and a black T-shirt, the few times I had seen the boy, he was always dressed in white pants and a T-shirt. Even though he'd been cut in *Palo* when he was barely five, he liked to wear the uniform of an initiate.

Now he was eleven, small but massive at four-feet-ten and a hundred and eighty pounds.

The bird on his shoulder had a parrot's magnificent head and the stiff sidelong look of a parrot, but its color was strange—it was all gray. Except for its blood-red tail feathers, and its black tree-branch feet, its whole body, except for its little eyes, looked like it had been dipped in ashes. It was a very judicious bird. It kept staring at me with that one-sided look of a parrot, in a very considering kind of way.

On the TV, an all-American-looking blonde girl twirled round in a long strapless black dress, hands on hips. Her family looked on, some with mouths open. Her brother, a muscular guy with a skinhead look in a long-sleeved plaid shirt, sobbed. His hands covered his face.

There was a cut to the way the girl used to look: fat and lumpy, no chin, bottle-lensed glasses. Mouthing: "They ser ah cun be purty." Then cut again to the girl in the black dress intoning with just a bit of Southern honey in her voice: "Why Jimmy, why are you crying, I'm beautiful now, aren't I?"

Both Genio and I were a little gape-jawed ourselves.

Finally, I said, "It's like they allowed her to be who she really was meant to be."

"That's what a makeover is," said Genio, his eyes still on the screen where now more of the girl's family were bursting hysterically into tears.

"We could both use a makeover, huh?" I couldn't help but guffaw.

Genio didn't seem to like to talk much and barely looked at me. But I thought that red glow in his dark eyes deepened as he watched the TV.

"AAAAAWK AWWKY," screamed the bird suddenly. "Makeover!" He moved his head side to side. Then again. "Makeover!" he squawked.

Genio giggled. "Wait a minute, I'll show you something." Genio got up from the TV armchair and went to his room.

The bird hadn't stopped studying me though. It was still turning its head from side to side.

"Wow," I said, "you are a parrot. You can talk great."

"TAAWK GREAT," the bird screamed. "TALK GREAT!"

"I'm sorry," I said to it. "I didn't mean to be rude."

Genio was back, and he was wearing a beautiful black hat. "Wow, a Fedora!"

Genio tipped the hat on his hand. "It's made of mink. It was Mami's. It has her name on the band inside."

"Can the bird understand everything?"

"EVERYTHING!" shouted the bird. "Makeover! Makeover!"

Genio tipped the hat again, and added a little twirl. Finally, he made quick eye contact with me, did a fumbling two-step and turned hot pink.

I suddenly realized that Genio was terribly shy. "Coco Loco likes you," he said softly.

There was a creaking noise, and a slit-eyed Victor reeled out of his bedroom and headed towards the kitchen.

Genio got up and said, "I got it, Pa." He stepped to the walk-in kitchen and quickly put water on to boil, then poured the boiling water into a coffee-filled sock placed on the rim of a bowl.

Victor went into the bathroom and turned on the shower, so I went to the kitchen and watched Genio beat sugar with a little bit of coffee in a porcelain coffee cup. It turned into a delicious caramel froth that he poured into the small white porcelain coffee cups.

I took a sip of the coffee. "I never had such good coffee," I said to the boy. "How do you make the topping so creamy?"

From the kitchen I looked at a painting on the wall of the tiny living room. It showed a black woman in a scant yellow top and skirt stepping into a river. Mama Chola, the river goddess.

The parrot said, "Cuban coffee!"

Genio patted the bird's leg. "You gotta beat it hard. A whisk is better."

"CUBAN COFFEE," screamed the bird. "CUBAN COFFEE!"

Genio pretended to ignore the bird that was now really trying to catch my eye and switching its head back and forth. It thrust out its beak, as black as obsidian, in a way that made me feel it might stab me with it.

I slurped down most of my coffee. We closed the door to the reading room behind us, and Genio whispered to me, "We can't give this bird coffee. Makes it shit all over the place. Papi says if it happens again, he's putting Coco Loco in a cauldron."

Victor sat mountain-like behind his table. I sat down in front of him. A large plastic basin stood on the floor next to the table. It contained three skulls in it, and I stared at them. The largest one was a sort of opaque white. Another one, the middle-sized one, looked a little waxy. The smallest one seemed different from the others—a larger forehead and eye sockets. I wondered if it was a woman's skull or a child's.

"They're from Haiti," Victor said, his voice a bit scratchy like a smoker's, but still dense like oil, too. "It's getting harder to have them brought to me intact."

I hesitated before I said, "The black wax *fufú* sort of worked. Technically speaking." I breathed out. "But I wasn't expecting this other woman. She just showed up."

"Maybe this Chico's not for you. Have you thought about that?" Tata searched my eyes.

I cleared my throat of the fury that was accumulating in it. "But I thought *Palo* could give me what I wanted?"

"You want something, but you don't want to give anything."

I took out a picture I'd printed out at work. It was Isis when she'd won the Miss Universe contest. In the picture she looked a little bit like Christy Turlington with honey-colored eyes and darker hair. "Can you do something with this?"

Tata looked at the picture, then chuckled. "I know her."

"You and everybody. She's a Puerto Rican Miss Universe."

"Not too famous to pay me a visit."

"Are you serious?" What the fuck? Next I'd be hearing that Chico had been coming to him for years for *fufús* to help him get gigs. "What did she want?"

He inclined his head slowly, his eyes staring me down. Isis Sandín was famous in her sphere, and he was famous in his. "Let's get to the nitty gritty here, girl. You've postponed the cutting. If you do the cutting, I'll start you on your own cauldron. Strong bones. Smell out whoever and drive them as far away as you want."

"Strong bones?"

"Almost as powerful as the Ancient One."

In the Ancient One's cauldron the thicket of *palos* looked as if they had been clumped together, blackening and gumming over, for hundreds of years. I couldn't see how Victor had extracted the moldy old thing from there.

I thought of that heaviness that had filled my stomach so that I felt like I never wanted to move again, of that voice that welled up out of me against my will. "I'm not ready for that. I can't do it."

A cough. Genio. "If she won't do it, can I do it, Pa?"

I turned towards him. He was standing behind me, one hand caressing the bird's feet, which looked like they were stabbing his shoulder through the T-shirt.

"There she is. Strong bones," said Genio. He took the hand off the bird's feet and pointed.

It was a small pot with just a few still green sapling *palos* in it. One of them was tied with a piece of yellow cloth.

"Nothing in it," I said.

"Everything that's powerful is under the *palos*," snapped Victor. "Feeding."

Then Genio lifted his slab-like arms and opened and closed his hands quickly, as if throwing something invisible at the small pot.

And then the small pot shook and rattled and slid across the room behind Victor's table.

Victor drawled in his dense and scratchy voice. "*Nene,* stop it. You can't have it. Not yet, anyway. Don't force it."

I got up to look, but I couldn't see the pot anywhere. "Where is it?"

A creaky laugh from Victor. "Just the kid up to his tricks. He can make these things invisible. Don't mean he was meant to master that pot."

The pot slid from behind Victor's table to its previous position about a foot in front of me.

The rattling started up again, and the bird squawked, "MAKEOVER. MAKEOVER."

Later that evening the girl was lying on my sofa in skimpy clothes watching *Spirited Away.* Shorts and a sleeveless tank top, nothing underneath. I could see the top of one of her light brown nipples. It looked like a hairless baby animal.

"Alba, your *tetas* are sticking out of your shirt."

"Huh?" The girl looked up from the cartoon.

I pointed at her nipple.

"Oh, sorry." She pulled haphazardly at the tank top, and now I could see both tits.

I went to the kitchen and came out with two plates of hamburger patties and rice and beans, put them on the glass coffee table and sat down.

"Did you go to rehearsal?" She had been hired to do a gig with Chico at Cleopatra's Needle and a few other places, and I'd heard her practicing. She was a great rollicking salsa songstress, but her voice could also dip into a well of velvety aching sadness, and now I knew what Chico meant when he had made that outlandish comparison to Hector Lavoe.

"Rehearsal got cancelled. Some big meeting or something."

"What kind of meeting?"

"Chico and a producer. Something like that."

"Do they want a record from him?"

The girl shrugged, then she looked at me. "I don't know. Maybe." Her eyes widened, and she sat up. "Ohmigod, maybe I can sing on his record!"

"Just as long as it don't interfere with school."

"School? You must be kidding! I'm done with school."

"How old are you, Alba?"

"Old enough to know I don't have to go back to that school in the Bronx no more. It looks like a jail, a big one, guards all over. And you don't learn shit 'cause it's like a hundred screaming kids in each class, and even the teacher can't hear herself." She rolled her eyes. "I was living with Jahaira and her guy, but they had to take in foster kids. The kids weren't terrible, but it was like the school. Jahaira had like ten of us to take care of, and I was just one of the pack. I left the day I turned eighteen."

"I'm sorry, Alba."

"It don't matter. Anyway, I'm going to be a good singer. My voice has gotten me more than a diploma from that dump in the Bronx."

"It's true you have a gift."

"I'm just a girl from somewhere. My roots go deep, somewhere out on the island. Somewhere I don't know at all. I gotta make myself, Fina, because if I don't, I'll die. I don't have anything to start with, so I could die right away."

"Don't say that."

Wasn't I a girl from somewhere, too? Nah, it was different. I had hated my sanctimonious old grandmother, but I had known the old bag. Known Barrio Sal Pa'fuera, its colors of every green in the world, its fragrance of night-blooming jasmine and that clay that smelled of shit.

"My singing is the only thing I got. I gotta protect it. Like a ring of power. Like the family jewels."

Alba stopped, then shrieked with laughter, amazed by the antics of a girl and a tall ghost in a subway car, the cartoon movie on the TV.

The sound of Alba's laughter suddenly bugged me a little. It was so . . . oblivious.

"You know, Alba. You can't stay for more than a few days."

She stopped laughing and frowned at me.

"Or maybe a week." She could stay the full week. No harm in that.

She sat up on the couch, blinked a few times, almost like she was going to burst into tears and then she put her shoes on and got up and walked to the door.

"Where are you going?"

"Upstairs."

"You can't go upstairs not wearing any underwear! What the hell are you trying to do? Break up Isis and Chico?"

"Like you give a shit." Alba's eyes emptied out, like the sockets in a cartoon character's face. When I went over and put a hand on her shoulder, she wiggled free.

"You don't get it!"

I crossed my arms over my chest. The girl's face turned a splotchy red. She started sobbing, but all the while, she kept pulling her hair over her eyes and mouth until her hair was all slobbered over with spit and tears. She smelled like hamburger and peanuts.

"Mami just disappeared all of a sudden without telling nobody nothing. Somewhere out on the island. Maybe she was murdered. Maybe my papi did it. Horrible, huh? Jahaira told me that. I don't really remember. I was a baby."

"But you thought Chico was your papi."

She rolled her eyes. "I know now that he ain't."

"Is that why you went to Tata Victor? To ask him?"

She looked away.

"Do you want to stay here tonight or not?"

"Look," she snarled, "Jahaira knows Victor. And she took me to see him because, yeah, I want to figure things out."

"So?"

"He ain't helping much. He wants me to, you know, commit to his freaking cult."

"What did he say about Chico?"

"That he ain't my papi. Like I freaking already told you."

Her usually chilling stare was softened by the tears. I had the sense that there was a part of her that wanted to break through and reveal things to me, but the demon seed in her wasn't having any of it.

"Just put a bra and panties on. Then you can go upstairs."

She glared at me, her face pale and her eyes again hollow-looking like skull sockets. From its place next to the sofa, she snatched up the gym bag containing her stuff and marched into the bathroom.

"Like loose titties is a crime or something," she muttered loud so I could hear; then she closed the door.

I was standing near Beltoff's inlaid wood desk as he sat circling mistakes as usual. His puffy pink skin looked scratched and irritated by his own ludicrous moustache.

When he finished marking up the pages, he said, "After you print out the final drafts, clean out your desk."

"What?"

He flushed slowly, that flush that most normal people would read as rage but which I now knew was just the happy anticipation that came to him when he knew he was causing pain, or about to cause it.

"You shouldn't have told Lori Shellman that she wouldn't be fired because I was afraid of her."

"So now you're firing me?"

"I'm demoting you to a sub-assistant position in the copy room."

He turned around and marched out of his own office, his head held high.

In the copy room, I made about one quarter of what I had made in the headmaster's office. Aside from the money problem, not being around Master Soul-Sucker was the bomb. And it wasn't too bad to have flunkies—the scholarship students—

to do the tedious work, and do it at an even faster clip than they were used to. In fact, the seeming setback was almost like a promotion to me.

So despite the fact that Beltoff had meant for me to do the copying itself, in my second week in the copy room, I ended up in a supervisory role. That's because I knew how to get work out of even the laziest and most bitch-ass of the scholarship students.

I started to discover that white kids were almost as leery about *brujería* as people of color. If they slacked off, I took to muttering over their shoulders about *fufús* and spells. They'd get back to their drudgery double *rápido*, still showing the whites of their eyes.

SIX

BIRTHDAY

At the spot Chico had set up for Isis' birthday party, I noticed an old lady, maybe Jewish, with cropped hair and cat-eye glasses reading a book on one of the park benches, next to a raisin-haired mulatto listening to his iPod. If the old lady had been passing through the projects, she would have bolted from the mulatto, his five heavy chains and his hands beringed in turquoise, coral and lapis. In the projects, the mean look on his face would have been a threat. On the park bench he was just local color, part of the idea that the neighborhood was finally integrating.

And maybe it was. Take the mama jama in short shorts shrinking up her cellulited thighs. She walked her toy poodle on the footbridge by the old waterfall. High up on one of her lumpy arms, circumscribed by a heart, was cursive: "*Te quiero, Pedro.*" Fat seemed to bubble like uncooked dough from under her tube top and panty-sized shorts, as she tiny-stepped behind the dog with pink bows on tail and topknot.

The mama jama lost grip on the pink suede leash, and the dog sprang away from her towards the down slope to the waterfall.

"Cleopachra!" she shouted after the poodle. "Cleo-pachra, honey princess, don't get your coat dirty."

The dog stopped on its hindquarters on a grassy knoll next to the water and started yipping.

A girl with a ponytail and in cut-off jeans knelt down next to the dog and patted her. "She's cute," said the girl, as the mama stepped gingerly down the slope reaching out her hands to steady herself on a boulder ruffled with lichen.

"My aunt has one like her," continued the girl. "My aunt's dog won every competition in Westchester County."

The mama jama tittered daintily as she scooped up the dog and pressed it to her ample chest. "My feeyancy bought Cleo from a breeder in Scarsdale."

"Your feewhat?"

"My feeyancy. Lookit." The mama put out a hand adorned with a ring.

"Nice," said the girl.

"He bought the dog from the best breeder in Scarsdale. Alma Everheart."

The teenager did a doubletake. "Ohmigod—that's my aunt!" Her blue eyes widened. "That dog is related to Supreme Grand Champion Duncan's Scarf Shimmering!"

"Yes, I know," said the mama, drawing herself to the lofty height befitting the owner of such a distinguished canine line.

When she ambled away from the mama, the girl's mouth was still making O's of surprise. She and the mama had something in common. And mama obviously thought that the dog was taking her places. What she couldn't see was that being the owner of Supreme Grand Champion Duncan's Whatever Whatever's grand pup would make a good "Ohmigod" anecdote for the girl. No more than that.

What made me different from the mama jama was my tasteful clothing—regular jeans and an Old Navy T-shirt sporting a witch on a broom. And my tattoos were artistic, unlike the mama's boring valentine to Pedro. People only got to see the lovebirds if I went bare-sleeved and bare-chested, and I only did that in private to tempt, or on purpose to provoke.

Above all, what made me different from the mama was my capacity for self-reflection.

But I sucked in my stomach anyway as I approached the tables Chico and the musicians had set up a few feet away from the uneasy couple on the park bench.

He was wearing a short-sleeved white linen shirt and khakis. He had a new haircut—all his grey hair had been skimmed off the top and the sides, leaving a dark layer of cropped hair that looked Roman. His hopeful eyes weren't bloodshot. But damn, what made me real uneasy was to see him without his rough and tough Nuyorican moustache.

"You couldn't wear one of your nice colored shirts?"

"Isis threw out all my old clothes and took me to Saks."

I gasped. "What about your lucky yellow pants?" I was indignant. Chico's outrageously colored clothes had a clown element, true, but they also worked. On him.

He chuckled. "Yup. Isis said those things were threadbare."

Chico had invited everybody that was local. His musician friends that lived on Duke Ellington Boulevard. Carlos, who owned the bodega on Amsterdam and 104th. Don Ramón, the Dominican who ran the dry cleaning store across from the project. And Perla, who came with her current boyfriend, a black former policeman, maybe fifteen years junior to her sixty-one. She met him in a math class she needed to take to help get her ready for Harlem College, which she planned to start at the end of the month. From the building, only I showed up.

On one of the tables sat pots filled with *arroz con pollo* and rice and beans, courtesy of Carlos. Chico had purchased a fancy strawberry cheesecake cake at the Silver Moon bakery on Broadway. On the cake, he'd put a large red and white "3" candle next to a "5." We all sang Happy Birthday in English, and then some of us sang it again in Spanish. Isis tried to extinguish the candle and wheezed like an old man.

"Yo, it's a trick candle," said one of the younger musicians. "It don't blow out."

Isis' face fell.

"*Bendito, mijo,*" I gave Chico a shove. "Now Isis won't get her wish."

"If the candle won't go out, maybe this happiness will last forever," said Isis, flashing her Miss Universe smile.

Don Ramón said "*Epa*," and people started kidding Chico and Isis about being in love like they were high school kids.

Only one of the musicians brought a gift, four bottles of Bacardi Limón that Chico mixed with lemonade and poured into disposable plastic cups filled to the rim with ice, so nobody got too happy. From Perla, Isis got a gigantic red beaded *candomblé* necklace from Brazil, more spectacular than *santería* necklaces. Isis put it on right away, and it looked like she'd wrapped herself in one of those plastic bead room dividers people used to hang up in the '70s. Don Ramón and his wife gave her a polyester sweater sewn through with gold metallic threads. I knew she would never wear it.

Alba gave her a weird bracelet made of little beads that looked like eyeballs. She said it was a necklace against the evil eye, but it looked like the opposite. Isis took hold of it like it was a dead rat and threw it in a Saks shopping bag somebody had brought.

My gift was a red and black beaded headband. I'd bought it at a 99-cent shop on 94th and Columbus. I had soaked it in a liquid infused with ground egg shell powder, mint, palm oil and *escoba amarga*.

I placed it on Isis' head. "Damn, too far back." I laughed and yanked it off with a few hairs. Isis cried out. I adjusted it.

"*Coño*, Fina," said one of the musicians. "Don't treat her so bad. She's got enough bad luck now that she's with Chico."

But the headband looked good on Isis, as I knew it would, bringing out the deep rose of her camisole and the reds in her flowered skirt. Hell, anything would have looked good on the homegirl, gotta give her that.

Isis' last gift was from Chico. It was one of those turquoise Tiffany's boxes. I held my breath. Isis undid the white ribbon, and pulled out a pair of earrings—woven gold knots—from the tissue.

I breathed out slowly. For homeboy that was breaking the bank.

It was hard to tell, though, what Isis thought. She looked up at Chico—her eyes faceted with all the colors between blue and brown—and said, "*Gracias, mi amor.*" The gushing didn't convince me. Wasn't it just a rich girl glow?

"There's something else," said Chico. And suddenly I was nervous for him. Without his smooth *Macho Camacho* moustache, he seemed too vulnerable.

Right there, in front of all the people who dealt with his basic needs, the last-minute food, the removal of questionable and tricky stains on his bright threads, the managing of cryptic ledgers, the supplies for my good work, the accompaniment to his own harmonies, he asked Isis to move in with him.

And Isis thanked him, just as she had for the earrings, covering up any real delight or disappointment. "*Gracias, mi amor.*"

Then she kissed him with an open mouth. Somebody called out "Was that a yes?" But they just kept on kissing.

When almost all of the picnickers had left the park, and Alba appeared out of nowhere to help the three of us clean up, Chico told me that although Isis wanted to give up her room in a suite at the Carlyle, she was still negotiating with her ex-husband.

"She gets me, and she gives up her right to inherit anything when he dies."

I cocked my head and looked into his eyes, but he didn't quite meet my gaze. "Does she get money now?"

"Oh, yeah, of course. It's part of the divorce." He half-smiled. "She gets something, he gets something. They're still working it out." In his beige linen shirt and pants, with hope widening his eyes, he looked like a grown-up boy scout.

That evening, Alba came by to get her things.

"What, you're not going to expose yourself on my couch no more?" I patted her on the shoulder, but her eyes got that weird rubber look, so I let go.

"I got shit to do, but I'll be back." She didn't have much stuff, some torn-up jockeys, a pair of jeans and T-shirts, which she put in a shopping bag.

After she closed the door, it occurred to me that she'd want to take my jar of peanuts with her, so I went out to the front of the building.

She was walking away from the building with a short guy with black hair. "Alba," I called out.

She looked back, and I waved the jar of Planter's at her.

The guy looked back, too. His face creeped me out. It was as white as a white worm's and saggy, even though there was tightness in the chin and around the eyes that might have been plastic surgery. He was fat and soft everywhere under his soft blue shirt and dark pants, and he waved and smiled, as cheerful as Santa Claus.

Alba shook her head, and she and her old-ass Romeo turned around and kept on walking.

SEVEN
A BIRD DEVOURED BY ANTS

I had hair from Isis' head. If you got a piece of your rival, why not turn it into a *fufú*? I am endlessly, tirelessly, creative that way.

Trouble was I couldn't get in touch with Victor. When I called his cell phone, the call went into voicemail right away. This happened for a few days in a row. I thought maybe he and Genio had gone to Miami for a few days, so I let it go.

In the meantime, Isis was spending most of her time with Chico.

One day I corralled her in the lobby. When she tried to squeeze past me, I told her I'd put a *fufú* on her unless she had coffee with me. She looked a little fish-mouthed, so I slapped her on the back, said I was joking, and that now was a good time for coffee because Alba wasn't around.

In my dining space, she said in her heavy but elegant island accent, "My husband hired him as the gardener. Were it not for that, I would not have met him. Somebody like that."

She chugged down her coffee, leaving little lipstick marks on the brim of the cup. I'd wipe those up later with tissue and add them to my growing stockpile.

"Were you a bored housewife watching soaps?"

"Fina, I was a star in these soap operas." Isis held out her empty cup.

I told her to go fuck herself in my thoughts, and filled her cup from the stovetop pot. "That was in that soap, *Matándote*, but they killed off your character, didn't they?"

"I could do a runway walk. But I could not act," Isis said. "I got bored. I had to repeat and repeat: 'Oh, Ricardo, don't leave me!'" Her arms reached out to an imaginary lover. "'What will I do now?'" She crumpled to her knees. She was right, she wasn't a convincing abandoned wife. Even when she knelt down, she looked proud and secretive.

"You look more like you're worried about the floor being clean."

"Alberto had a mistress. When I pretended to play a scorned wife on TV, maybe it hit me . . . too close. I . . . how do you say . . . froz-ed. I could not say, '*No me dejes*,' since I was thinking it all the time." She got up from her knees, and sat in one of the dinette chairs.

"Did he tell you about it?"

Isis cupped her chin in her hand and closed her eyes.

"I kissed him one day." She twisted her mouth. "That is how I knew."

"What?"

"He tasted like the beach. Have you been to the beach on the Condado? Right before sunset?"

"I grew up out on the island," I said, suddenly ashamed of naming Barrio Sal Pa'fuera. Nobody from the island I had met in New York had ever heard of it. If you weren't from a town proper, but only from the outlying barrios, people had your snapshot: clay hillsides, zinc-roofed wooden shacks, barefoot girl leading a goat, boy fucking a cow at night.

"The seaweed has piled up really high on the sand by that hour. It smells like garbage. Maybe it is the sewer water coming out from the hotels. Or the chemicals the pharmaceutical companies dump in the ocean. Maybe both." Her nostrils flared.

"If you step on the seaweed," Isis continued, "you get swarmed by these, these, I don't know what they call them, they are like gnats that bite hard."

"I swam in the rivers, not the beaches," I said. "The only thing I worried about was snails in the water because that meant there was Bilharzia."

She tipped her head, not too interested in the rivers of my childhood. "When he kissed me he smelled like that, like the beach with the gnat-filled seaweed." She looked at me with moist eyes. "Like pussy." Her accent made the word hiss.

I raised my eyebrows. "So what did you do?"

"I told my mother what I was thinking. She says to me that it is true. Can you believe that? My mother knew he had other women. Even before we were married."

"What did she say?"

"Something stupid: '*Ay* Isisita, all men have their *queridas, mija*. When you're older you'll appreciate not having to open your legs all the time.'" Isis pulled a lock of hair over her mouth. "I learned Papi had a mistress too, and that it was a relief for Mami. Mami had more feelings for the maid than she had for my Papi. The maid was the one who took care of Mami when she had her *ataques*."

After she heard out her mother, she drove fast through the island's old highway, dizzied by the curves in the mountains. She looked out the BMW's window, and wondered what it would be like if she drove the silver car over the cliff. *Would he love her better dead? Should she come back and love him better dead?*

She said that she parked the car a few blocks away from the house. It was early evening. Nobody outside. She saw a light in one of the bedroom windows. Not their bedroom. She unlocked the door—one of those mahogany doors with con-quistadors and palm trees carved all over it. Heavy and dark, like all the furniture in the house.

The Ferrera house frightened her. Unlike her family's zinc-roofed house in Vega Baja, to which succeeding generations of Sandíns added rooms in a ramshackle way, the Ferrera house was born of her husband Alberto's desire to unite the best features of a colonial plantation big house and a Spanish fortress.

He paid a French architect a fabulous sum to carry out his idea. Mahogany-beamed ceilings on the first floor. Narrow windows, like those in the lookout towers of El Morro, adorned the living room, the piano room, Alberto's study and even the pool room on the first floor. Only the kitchen, modeled after one Alberto had seen in an old coffee plantation house in Dominica, had large windows that the early morning light turned lemon and orange.

It felt like the light was hugging her when Isis sat at the kitchen table in the mornings to read magazines or talk about the day's menus with Margarita, the cook. The windows' shutters had been fashioned from Ceiba wood, unlike the mahogany used in the rest of the house. The bedrooms, of which the house had many, had larger windows and enormous closets. The master bedroom even had a room-sized balcony. But Isis felt lonely sitting there, haunted by the wind blowing through the mango trees. She always went back to the kitchen.

That night when she entered the house, it was quiet, except for a knocking noise: a taca, taca, taca coming from the third floor. The house was dark except for the bedroom that was not her bedroom. Taca, taca, taca. Like someone was killing a cockroach over and over again.

Isis started up the stairs. She had never realized before how long and wide those stairs were. The door of their bedroom was open. Alberto laughed, and a woman moaned. Then there was a third voice. He was there with two women!

In her imaginings of this moment she had seen herself screaming up the stairs. But now it was as if she were mute. And she could barely breathe.

Isis peeked in and nobody noticed her, as they were too absorbed in each other. One woman was under Alberto, and the other one was next to him on the bed. The one under him was dark-haired. She was small with big breasts and hips that were out of proportion to the rest of her body. Her skin was darker than Isis'. The one next to him looked like a *gringa*. The darker one had hair the same color as Isis' hair, but different.

That thick hair of an animal. Her skin was like coffee, with a lot of milk in it. The way Alberto liked to drink it. And he sure was drinking it now, thrusting into the dark woman so violently the bed was making that taca noise again. Their own expensive bed never made much noise!

The *gringa*, a blonde with a pixie haircut, lay on her side watching the other two. She was very young and boyish in everything—tall, small-breasted with Raisinet nipples and straight hips—except the sex which was fair and wispy, and out of which dropped a little plump rosebud of a clitoris that she played with absent-mindedly. Her body was stretched out like a cat that's just eaten, so Isis thought maybe she had just been taken.

But it was the one he was fucking that he liked, that was clear to Isis. The one who was what he often praised: a *criolla* with meat on her bones.

I had been very quiet, but now for the first time, I felt the sudden furnace of a blush, and I made some sort of incoherent noise.

Isis looked at me, her eyes a cool green. "Her sex was wide open. Like those flowers that all the insects go into. That *puta*."

That was why the *criolla* kept her pussy up in the air like that. She knew it was irresistible. It was like she was saying, come taste my night flower, Papi. Alberto couldn't help himself . . . he got under her and drank her dew. The blonde tried to touch them, but they weren't paying any attention to *her*. Then Alberto entered the little one from behind her wide ass. Isis had never seen his behind from that angle before, the balls hanging like plums. Those two were so in tune with each other that they gasped at the same time.

Isis gasped too and crumpled to her knees in the hallway, just outside the bedroom door. The boy-girl started kissing the *morena*'s mouth and playing with one of the dark woman's purple-tipped breasts, while the man kneaded the *morena*'s other breast as if to anchor himself deeper. Alberto humped and cursed and called the *morena* his whore in Spanish. "*¡Puta! ¡Qué puta!*"

And the *morena*, agreeing she was a *puta*, his *puta*, begged for her papi to split her open. Isis heard the *morena* lullaby a stream of demands: *dame bicho, párteme, ábreme, guáyame el bumper, rómpeme la crica, dame leche.* Then Alberto told the *gringa* to scoot her ass down on the bed. He pushed the *morena*'s face into the girl's crotch.

Alberto said in English, "*Puta*, you can't get enough, can you? Now you're getting it from both sides!" The *morena* slipped two fingers and her tongue inside the girl. "You're always ready to be fucked, you're always willing to take dick and suck cunt," Alberto said, and the *morena* said, "Oh, yes, Papi, yes."

Her sigh was almost a sob before she continued, "I'll take your animal whenever you want, and suck any pussy you like!" Then the blonde girl, who had been quiet, released a jagged cry. Isis could smell the sudden hot vapor that rose from the bed, a sweat of bay rum, cooked meat, bodily fluids. Isis covered her mouth with a hand, finding that she wanted to cry out too.

She broke into a cold sweat, her thighs shivering. She thought she was going to faint. She put a hand up her dress, her panties were soaked and her pussy was still pulsing hard and painfully from her own orgasm.

They napped and she rested too, before slipping quietly out of the house.

I looked at her, and she looked at me. "You want to know why I did not tell Chico that you were in his closet that night?"

I snorted because I knew what she was going to say.

"Because you are like me," said Isis.

I stared at her stonily, unable to deny it.

Once outside the house, Isis stopped on the patio, forgetting for a moment where she was headed. She looked down to get her bearings and saw a bird in the grass right next to the paved stones. She saw by the twist of its neck that it was dead. It might have been a pigeon, but that was hard to tell, because it was covered so completely with ants, it looked like it was vibrating. There were five long lines of ants radiating from it. One of the lines was so long it curled around the patio and into the shrubs leading to the neighbor's patio. The blackened bird looked alive as it pulsed there at her feet. Terribly alive.

EIGHT
THE DARKNESS UNDER

T he thugs who usually hung out on the front steps were milling around the lobby with one or two of their high-strung Wall Street amigos. When I tried to get to Victor's door, a wiry kid with green eyes and a keloid scar on his forehead pushed me. I elbowed him in the gut only to find, when I finally made it inside Victor's apartment, even more of a crowd.

But this time it was men in white shirts and women in flouncy skirts and white bandannas. There was a blondish man in jeans, sneakers and a leather jacket talking to a short black guy in an initiate's cap and white pants and shirt.

The blondish man was taking notes in a little battered notebook. I recognized the short black guy as Niño, one of Victor's godchildren. He had a heart containing a big "N" tattooed on an upper arm. I always wondered whether the "N" stood for his name or for the Ñetas, one of them prison gangs that do things like skin "rats" alive and send the skin wrapped as a present to the victims' families.

The fair-haired man closed his notebook and put it away in an inner jacket pocket. He looked around the hallway, where people were pointedly trying not to make eye contact with him.

Rapapapap. Disturbing, but rhythmic. Was it a kind of drumming?

"Are they playing the *cajón* in there?" I asked a tall woman with pale skin and bloodshot eyes who blocked my way. She finally let me pass. The rhythmic rattling noise was definitely coming from the reading room, but the door to it was closed.

I breathed in the scent of dried blood in the air, the iron in it and the sweetness.

The deep clanking noise stopped as soon as the tall woman closed the door to the apartment.

"*Nkisis* acting up in the reading room?"

"You're Josefina, right?" said the woman.

"Where's Tata Victor?"

"I'm Dalia." She led me past the reading room along the hallway.

The man with the little notebook squeezed past us and left the apartment.

On the TV, a British woman with rhinestone-rimmed cat-eye glasses described the procedure for deviling eggs.

Niño was now sitting on the couch looking at the TV. When he saw me, he got up, came over and threw his arms around me.

"Girl! Where you been? You coulda helped cook or something to get us through this shit."

Dalia sat down on the plastic-covered sofa. "That cop finally hit the road." She started rubbing at her eyes.

"Is Tata in bed? Is he sick?" I asked. I was bewildered.

Real tears started rolling down Dalia's face. One of Niño's eyes started a mad twitching, and he sat back on the sofa.

Behind the closed door of the reading room, something heavy crashed to the ground and split apart. Then the smell of gunpowder seared the older, mustier, smells of blood and earth in the apartment.

Dalia sprang up, throwing her arms in the air. "I can't. I can't. I can't anymore," Dalia shouted. "No more!"

Niño called over a man in an initiate's cap, who was hanging out in the hallway, and had him take Dalia by the arm into the building lobby.

Rapapapap. Insistent. Loud. Then it stopped.

"What the hell is going on?"

"Eugenio is gone," said Niño.

"Eugenio?" Genio. "Gone. You mean he left? What happened?"

"He was alone here. Tata had gone out to do an *ebbó* for a baby that was dying. And somebody . . . "

"Is he okay?"

Niño closed his eyes and covered his mouth with a hand. "They used a machete from one of the cauldrons."

I gasped. "He's dead?"

There was a muffled sound behind the door, different from the rattling, like a simple shift or beat of energy. Not quite movement. A presence behind the door. But in the past the presences—the *nkisis*, *ndokis* and *nfuiri* spirits that answered to Victor—quieted and rumbled at his bidding.

Spetetata. Like fire spitting.

"Can I see Victor?" I started down the hallway.

Niño got up from the couch, came after me and grabbed my hand.

I let him stop me. Pint-size really couldn't have held me back once I was in freight train mode.

"There's nobody in there," said Niño. "Don't go in. You can't handle this stuff."

"What do you mean?"

"Victor told me you can't . . . "

The doorknob of the reading room turned. Slowly, yes, slowly. Then it was still. The back of my neck started to itch.

Niño pretended he hadn't noticed the moving doorknob. "I think we need to wait for Tata before we go into the reading room. The detective spoke to him, then Tata went back to his room." Niño walked back to the living room. From where I stood, I saw him sit back on the couch and pretend to train his eyes on the TV.

The people in the hallway cleared out; Dalia or whoever went home, and the English TV cook's techniques made Niño snore. But Victor still wouldn't come out of the bedroom.

Genio dead? That obese but sensitive kid cut down with a machete? Not just a *palero*'s son, but a *palero* himself.

I stood outside of Victor's bedroom and was about to knock when I heard that rattling sound, again, but it was quick, like the sound of thrown dice.

I moved on down the hall, again, to the reading room. I looked at the doorknob. It looked okay. I pressed my ear to the door, and didn't hear a sound. Then I opened the door.

Nothing there. Or nothing compared to what had been there before. None of the cauldrons bristling with their ram's horns, monkey skulls, hatchets, machetes, handcuffs and blackened spears. Just red dirt scattered all over the linoleum; sticks of wood, chips and grayish chunks of what seemed like bones, and unidentifiable gray, brown and blue powders.

The door shut behind me.

I turned to open it, but I couldn't. I shook the doorknob, and then the rattling started up again.

Rapapap. It was coming from next to me, but I couldn't see what was making the sound. Instead of running, my hips swayed, one leg stepped forward and I started to dance, Rapa, my hip, Papap, my breast, Papap, my legs. Rapapapap curling deep in my body. Rapapapapapapa. The death rattle of the rooster. Rapapapapapap. By the river. *It dies so you can live.* Rapapapap. The hurricane waters that fell like a firing squad on the zinc roof the night Papi left. "Fill the *bóveda* glasses for me, *nena.*" Because there was death in this power and above all power in death . . .

Rapapap. The gnashing sound of fire. I closed my eyes, and when I opened them, the little cauldron with its *palos* of green wood stood at my feet. One of the *palos* was tied with a faded yellow ribbon.

I knelt down on the floor. A chunk of something crunched under my knee. I patted the tops of the green wood sticks coming out of the baby cauldron. One of the pieces of wood was razor sharp and cut my finger. I pulled my hand away quick, and a drop of blood fell onto a green *palo*. I licked my finger, and the pot rocked from side to side.

I kept my hands on the iron, warm to my touch.

The pot's rattling wound down to a humming, and it stopped moving altogether, and then there was a banging on the door and an indistinct cry of rage or pain. The door flew open. Victor's hair puffed out like a black lion's; his eyes bore into mine and the gray parrot perched on his shoulder dipped its head and squawked. Its raucous cries deepened the howling that seemed to come from behind and outside of Tata Victor, a wind surging and whistling in that narrow room, and rushing over the cauldron.

I took a few steps towards him, and he stopped, took deep breaths and watched me. Finally he thundered, "What did you do?"

I found that I couldn't budge one of my legs. I could move my upper body, but my right leg was rooted to the ground. "I can't move."

"MOVE!" squawked the bird. "MOVE, FINA!"

I tried again to move and my left leg fumbled forward, but my right leg seemed to plant itself even more firmly, and I felt the strangest sensation as if it was shaking into the floor beyond it.

"I can't move, Tata. Please. Help me." It was coming to take me, a numbness taking hold of my leg, and now the swoon again.

Victor snarled and lurched towards me, and the bird raised its wings. He brought his hands up to his hair and tore at it. "Genio was my son!" His eyes were bloodshot, and when he brought the fingers of one hand away from his head they were clutching a clump of his own hair. The bird squawked and Victor let go of the bloodied clumps of hair, which fell like tiny wounded animals to his feet.

"I'm sorry, Tata, so, so . . . " What did I want to say? My body was moving away, it was going somewhere else. My mind was going too . . .

He closed his eyes and opened them and hissed. "You must have done something. What did you do?"

"DO, DO, DO!" shouted the bird. "FINA, DO!"

"I'm sorry, Tata, but I touched it. I touched a *palo*, and I cut myself on it."

My feet were rooted, my hands blossomed upward. I was a tree born of a river.

"You fed it? You mean it showed itself to you?"

Victor grabbed me by the shoulders and breathed hot air into my face while Coco Loco lifted his wings and took off in a circle around the room squawking, "FINA FED IT! FINA! FINA DID IT!"

I swooned deeper, knowing that beyond the vertigo there was relief. For a moment, Tata's eyes looked like fuzzy brown pansies. I closed my eyes, and I remembered the river in Barrio Sal Pa'fuera, the silver water. On walks with my father, I had looked at the surface many times. Now I was seeing the darkness, the darkness of caves under the mountains that winded finally down to the rivers, the darkness where the spirits lived.

"Genio did his trick." Tata narrowed his eyes. "The cauldron went invisible. Even I couldn't see it. That's how it escaped the bastard that I'm going to kill. Fina, they hacked my boy from head to shoulders."

Victor looked away, tried to speak, but his voice caught. Finally he said. "His mother collapsed when she saw him. She's in the hospital. It's going to kill her." And Victor staggered towards his chair, placed his elbows on the reading table, looked down at the divination *cobos* and shells and started sobbing. "He was the best son, the best anyone could have."

I held out my arms helplessly, but I stumbled. I couldn't reach the table.

The bird cocked its head and stared. "HELLO, FINA! GENIO LIKED FINA!"

I remembered crouching next to Papi at the river's edge. Papi pointed to a tiny plant. I could hardly see it among the weeds and grass of the riverbank. "*Nena linda*," his voice pitched deep, "this is the life-death plant. Brush your fingers over it." I touched its delicate leaves. Each purplish leaf folded like tiny wings. I tried to pull open one of the leaves with my babyish fingers. "It's the *morivivi*, Finita. It opens and lives, and closes and dies, and then it lives again." Papi's voice was soothing, yet electric.

"It's asleep?" I asked.

"When it's ready, it will wake from its sleep. And sometimes that can happen with the dead. The life-death plant. Remember, *nena*, to fill the *bóveda* glasses, keep them filled with water for me."

The river, the caves under the mountain, to go underwater now . . . I was damned alert too, as if a light had been switched on in my brain. But it was somebody else's light. Somebody else was here with me . . . Papi? Not Papi. Death in the water. Death would quench the stifling, the dizziness, the weird alertness. The body, the burning, the shooting, the fire—all that would go if I let it take me.

What does fire sound like when you hear it from a distance, as in a deep dark dream?

Fire? What fire? I opened my eyes, but I was still dizzy. *It's the life-death plant, it dies to live again.*

I drank air like water. "I'm not falling into the river," I cried out. But it was in the water that they waited. My father, the others. Waiting to be called forth, waiting for time and words. The bones of my power.

"I will take you with me. Stay with you. Fill the *bóveda* glasses for me. Then I will be free."

"I keep the *bóveda* glasses filled with water for all my dead."

"And then one day take the bones to the water."

"I will. If I can find them, if I can find you, I will. I will take your bones to the water. But let me go for now."

And what had grabbed hold of me pulled back, and I was free again, and fell in Tata Victor's arms.

"The *nfuiri* in that pot grabbed you by the leg."

He held me, and we were both cold and muddy with sweat, but I was feeling strangely serene, too, like I'd come up through a swamp to face the sun, and the bird was squawking, flying around the room, its flapping wings sounding like a hundred birds flocking into the mountain's caves.

"I want to be cut," I said.

"SHE WANTS IT!" cried Coco, landing on my shoulder, his sharp talons helping to bring me back, so I stood up straighter. "NOW SHE'S READY!"

The set of Victor's face was still grim, with the rage he was nursing to keep it warm; but at least his eyes were dark and filled with burgundy lights again. "I know."

PART TWO

PART TWO

ONE

OUT OF THE FOREST

I gotta track back now to tell *her* part of the story, the part of the story that's before and after. Before she was an *nfuiri* . . . but after she was a woman. Because later I remembered it all, those memories that weren't even mine. The part of her story that came way before she grabbed a hold of my leg, and before I was cut.

What did the fire sound like? It sounded like house-sized jaws chewing a million needle-boned squirmy rodents, one after the other, breaking their necks, sucking out their entrails.

It was a scary, long, slow crescendo.

And then the explosion. The melting of skin, the singing of blood, the grinding of bones. That body? Was it her body? Lick, lick, lick, the fire lapped up the juice, the plump sun of what had been her body, leaving charred scraps of bones.

A skull webbed with hissing fat.

The spirit was still trapped, though. She fluttered around the chips of the bones like a torn dress trying to let the wind carry her off. She heaved and pulled but she was as stuck as the dried fat to those bones.

In the early morning of the first days she writhed like a snake, dry and thirsty, although she had no memory of what she was thirsty for. She could hear the swallows fly to the caves, the wasps zing off to their nests. She could even hear the roots of the Ceiba stir again, the seeds of the grasses sprout, the worms shitting as they rolled around her . . . So many tiny noises increasing with the sun to noon. Then the heat drew out a ringing silence, and she was only the dry hot rubble that grated against the even drier clay of the earth.

When night came, the pressure inside the skull decreased. She expanded as far as she could, sensing, although unable to leave those broken bones, the ocean of night and possibility.

She breathed the blue cool nights in and out with such desire that one evening, along the procession of the years, she found herself outside the bones. The ceaseless rainwater of a hurricane flooded the remains and sent the skull rolling away from the pile of shards and slivers. The tattered dress of her spirit flew off over the burned out ruins of a shelter of some sort, made of wood and zinc. She surveyed the tops of the Ceiba trees, the occasional silver shimmer of *yagua* leaves in the sun, the night flight of swallows and bats, the pattering of rats in grass.

The world was clear, dripping wet with bright greens and blues.

For hours, she floated in the air surveying it all, wondering, attempting to know it. Then the sky, the mountain, the forest, the palpitating disc of the sun ceased to satisfy her as things in and of themselves. She was aware that plants and flowers came into leaf, died, then grew again. The animals were born, and then died, and did not come back again. She too had grown. But from where? What nest? What body?

The spirit, who really couldn't think properly at that point, tried to understand. Was she born from the fire? What had come before that? Darkness? And before that? What was the connection between these things that existed, the darkness behind her and her restlessness?

She tried to cry out but she had no voice at all, and the cool wind over the mountain swallowed her soundless screams.

A *yagua* leaf fluttered to the ground. She swooped down and entered a rat.

A body! What a trip it was to have even a small floppy little body. Now she could feel more. She scuttled along the damp floor of the forest, devouring offal and spoiled fruit, reveling in a myriad of tiny smells, feeling the little sharp bones in her mouth grind up the refuse, and calm and fatten her body.

And now there was a pinprick, a disturbance, a tiny tear in the fabric of eternity through which she fleetingly perceived the past, of which she had no memory. Or did she? And the future was proven only because there was a tear in the continuous fabric of forest, mountain and sky.

But after a while the rat bored her. A rat could not move or fly as a spirit floating. A rat was afraid of too many things.

She entered a bat, which plunged quickly into the velvety mouth of one of the mountain's caves. The bat hurtled through a long dark tunnel, and a lighter shadow grew like a haze in the distance. Then she was blinded by windy light at the cave mouth. The bat resisted her, so she flung it like a rock into the sparkling air. A thousand feet over the silver river and the green valley and the galloping clouds, she reeled maniacally in the air. Before, she had floated dozens of feet over the ground. Now she was thrilled by such never-before-achieved height, dazzled by the sensation of speed and fear and wonder in a body.

Against her attempts to direct it higher and higher, to explode the limits of its wiry body, the bat screeched in high-pitched tones. In terror, the other bats and swallows in the cave mouths on that side of the mountain thundered into the air. Ekayaka Kayaka Ekaya Kayaka screamed the bats. Kaya Caya Caya. Ya . . . ¡Calla ya! For a moment the noise recalled something, something distant. ¡Calla ya! Rage! Calla, calla, ¡calla ya! She went on wheeling about in the frigging air. ¡Calla ya! ¡Cállate ya! It was a rage deep inside her, a rage rooted in another world.

But when the whirring of a million wings blew away, she lost interest in the bat and hurtled from its body, floating low over the river. Where did that river go? Was there an animal who would take her beyond the end of the river?

Mournfully, she entered a mongoose, but the creature was filled with a burning thirst, and choked every time it tried to drink river water. Ay Awwowrita Reekiti Reekiti Rekeeti. Ay Awwowrita Ri ta Ri ta Ri ta Ri . . . Ay Rita ri Rita. Ay Aw Rita ritari. Ritari? The sorrow, the loss, the betrayal. Who had betrayed her? What being had she been, so filled with sorrow and rage, so easily betrayed?

After that, she entered all the creatures that ranged over the rainforest and the mountain and that lived in the inkiest pools of the caves. She searched in their noises for a meaning that was lost to her. Not that she understood in those days what that might be. She knew only in moments of feeling, and even tinier flashes of memory. Was she now unique in existence, a being that had never owned a body?

And then one day, the human came. When she saw him she knew he was human. She knew he was a man. She saw again those other eyes. She knew that she had known humans. She did not know how. It was a vague memory, from before the dreams of fire.

When she tried to remember, she lost her way. Just as a swallow can lose its way in the mountain's hollow caves, wandering in the places that are deep, unknown and shadowless. In the cold windless air the bird's flying turns eventually to stone.

This man loomed like a hill. His eyes were sharp like a rat's. He had black hair, and arms as thick as tree branches. He searched the ruins, but his purpose seemed more meaningful than that of scavengers. He poked around in the grass with a strange, long, polished stick.

He picked up the blackened skull and blew over it with his red lips. From her dreamy meandering among the clouds, she felt his call. Her spirit hovered near him. She covered his large body like a shadow. He sensed her more keenly than the animals in the forest.

He put out his hand and spoke to her. "*Tie tie masimene. Aquí hay huesos de nganga, una muerte maléfica. Tu trabaja pa' mí y yo trabajo tu bien.*"

The spirit did not understand, she only felt. He seemed to promise her rest.

He had come from the valley or beyond, perhaps from even beyond the river. Had she too once traveled beyond the river? She recalled suddenly that in the dreams of fire she had seen human faces, mask-like with hate. *Quémale la cara, quémala.* Then a brand flying, then falling.

Fascinated by this tear in the fabric, she slipped into the man. She tried to move him around like those other puppets—the rodents and birds. But the man turned and spoke more words and unlike the bat, the rat, the mongoose, the man took the spirit that she had poured into his body and flung it right out of himself like a rabid mongoose vomiting river water.

He took off parts of his feet—she did not know then what shoes were. He tied a blade of grass on one of his toes. Then he flung open his hands and grasped her floating, aimless, spirit and cradled it as if he could feel it. This moved her. No other creature had held her in so loving an embrace.

"Una casa para tu descanso. Una casa para tu reino. Una casa en mi casa." He spoke words that told her she would have form, words that said she would have answers. Above all he promised her rest . . . a home. *Una casa en mi casa.*

Instead of pushing and pulling at him, driving his body into the forest filled with wasp's nests, or the cliff's edge over the river, she let go. And he took her weak spirit and wrung it tightly with his hands, his words and his will, before coiling it back into her skull. And then he threw the blackened skull, and what was left of her bones and the dirt in which she'd been buried, into a raffia sack.

Tú reinas en mi casa, yo reino en ti.

Later, much later, I think, the spirit heard another voice, another human voice: eager, sharp, insistent. *"¿La encontraste?* The bones . . . were they there?"

That was at the stopover in Barrio Trastalleres in San Juan. At that point, dumped in a bag like she was special garbage, could she recognize her own sister's voice? Her sister Jahaira who knew enough to know where the bones were. I don't think so. She didn't have the capacity. She wasn't helped yet. . . .

"*La encontré.* I found her but just part of the skull, and some burnt bones, that was all that was left."

"I haven't gone there for a long time."

"She wasn't even buried anymore, Jahaira. Hurricane waters, whatnot."

"You got enough, you got enough. I'm gonna call the kid."

"No. Knock it off, Jahaira. She's too . . . you know. She's not cut, she's not even called. She shouldn't be part of the making of an *nganga*. Especially not this one."

Tú reinas en mi casa, yo reino en ti.

That was all she knew. She would do his bidding. In turn, her desire would be fed, she would increase in knowledge.

And she would know again what she had known so long ago.

TWO

THE CHARRED HANDS

If you're some kind of supernatural being, used to floating over a mythical forest where every Ceiba tree has a wasp's nest as big as a piñata hanging from it, a Spanish Harlem apartment can really cramp your style. Hell, a Spanish Harlem apartment with just two windows in the whole place could cramp anybody's style. Still, even the spirit could tell that Victor and Genio had gone out of their way to recreate a bush ambiance, so to speak. The *palos* of bamboo, mahogany, Ceiba and palm in the iron cauldrons . . . yeah, they reminded the spirit of the forest. A little. And there were other things that she recognized: *guaraguao* and *pitirre* feathers. *Yagua* leaves. Dirt of course. Bones.

She smelled herbs. And that sweet rotting smell of old animal blood.

But then there was a subtle shift of energy in the room. And then something like a silent whisper. She realized that, okay, so there weren't a helluva lot of flowers and live grass here. But there were more . . .

In that room, there were more like her.

The voices spoke to her so that Victor and the boy couldn't hear. At first the spirit could barely hear those others. The first thing the voices said was that she was not alone. In this place of grayness, of roads that wound endlessly into more roads and never-ending masses of men, there were spirits everywhere.

Many spirits barely lived in this city that had forgotten them. They waited silently for the words, the rituals, the sudden understanding that would bring them back. Let them ascend. And then finally go.

The *nfuiris* in the cauldrons told fragments of stories of bodies that had died. Stories that were like hers in one way. They had died violently. They had been murdered.

And now they were *nfuiris* belonging to Tata Victor Tumba Fuego, master of *ngangas.*

They got a little excited. For *nfuiris* that is. Whispering still, but now also starting to spit, they told her that it was the work they did for Tumba Fuego that would free them.

"*Free . . . To have a body?*" asked the spirit

"*To die!*" said the *nfuiri* of a child.

An evil man had tortured the child, had cut its throat and buried its body in a building near Tumba Fuego's. A follower of Tumba Fuego's had detached the femur of the dead child's leg, and its skull. I don't even want to know how. It was this tortured child's spirit that reigned in one of the largest cauldrons. Tata Victor used the child *nfuiri* for his most perilous deeds.

"*To die, finally!*" hissed the child. "*To die from a death that was no death.*"

"*To live in heaven!*" said another.

"*There is no heaven, fool,*" said the Ancient One. He was more than three hundred years old, and in life had been a great sorcerer, a slave tortured to death for inciting slaves to rebel. His head had been rescued by Tumba Fuego's ancestor and had spoken since then to the rescuer's descendants. He was more than an *nfuiri*, much more.

"*And especially not for us,*" said a robber who had been shot by his victim. The "secret" in his cauldron had been made from his knucklebones.

"Papi, it's getting hot in here." The fat boy wiped his brow. "This spirit has enough *aché* to shift the energy, huh?"

"*Will the man help us?*" She asked the *nfuiris.*

"*Help us? The man rules over us,*" said the robber.

"*Slaves. We are slaves,*" lamented the *nfuiri* of a woman who had drowned in an artificial lake, in a forest that was made by the men of the city.

"*Fools! We are slaves who have unique power. We are slaves who can enslave those who would use us.*" The Ancient One expanded in his cauldron like a shadow on a wall. Then he shot out energy like a blow, and the spirit could no longer hear the hissing of the others.

"*You can know more,*" said the Ancient One. "*You have enough* aché *to know more.*"

But she could not respond to him. Didn't know how yet or maybe he was too powerful and wouldn't let her. He was strong, and he wanted her to know it.

And yet, she began to realize that she was strong too, stronger than the others, except for the Ancient One.

He took the attitude of a scary elder, and she was the gifted, if still clueless, young one. She knew right away because at a certain point the Ancient One was talking just to her, and not to the others.

"*You can know more in time, but now is not the time.*"

"Can I bring Coco Loco in?" said the boy.

"It's getting late. I don't want to wait for that girl to come by and make her crazy demands. I want to start now."

The boy grunted and left the room. The man lay down on the floor of the room filled with the cauldrons.

"*He will make you now,*" said the Ancient One, in his grandiloquent way. "*He will make you his slave. He will make you his slave of power, but it is a power that you will also have over him.*"

"*Why does he lie on the floor?*" The *nfuiri* asked the Ancient One.

The Ancient One, bored with her questions, vanished to some unknown level of privacy, but two of the others hissed suddenly, "*It is earth. Because it is the earth. The source.*"

"*It is the earth that nourishes his magic,*" said the Ancient One finally. "*And this cold floor is what is closest to the earth.*"

The boy came back with a white sheet and covered the man's body. Then he lighted tapers in metal holders and placed them at the man's feet and near his head.

The spirit could feel the energy in the room change, as if the other entities were shifting in the dirt of their pots, and fully stirring.

The boy placed seven small heaps of black powder on the long blade of a knife, and set the blade on the floor next to the man. The boy flailed his arms around, and the spirit was baffled, but then she realized he was speaking to her, shouting, haranguing, asking her to work for the man.

She remembered almost longingly how the man had cradled her in the forest, had comforted her, and because she wanted to feel his embrace again, she entered his body.

The seven heaps of powder on the knife exploded. The *nfuiris* in the cauldrons, tied like strips of black cloth to the earth of their prisons, leapt high. They touched her lightly as she rode the man.

He did not fling her out, as he had before, and maybe that sudden sense of her power gave the spirit a few ideas. She plummeted into his being with gusto.

The man had made the small room his mountain. He controlled the *nfuiris* in their cauldrons, even the *nkisis*, who were much greater than the dead, and to some extent the boy. His vision cut at an angle, seeing the boy, the phantom forest of sticks and cauldrons, the sweating window to the street, the thugs and their clients.

They went further into memory. Mist wrapped around trees. A tall woman whose face she could not see poured gasoline on a body, and lit it with a match. Flowers of fire blew into the air consuming the body, the ground, the plants, the insects and the earth around the body.

The scorched body lay on the ground, and the burned hands reached into the air. The hands jumped, the fingers like red tentacles still snatched at life, although the body was dead. And other hands shoveled earth over those moving hands. But the hands continued to claw up through the earth. The dirt shoveled over them couldn't cover them, and there was a gasping sob.

The shovel was thrown down, and the sobbing faded into the distance.

Eventually the charred hands, ribboned with blood, stopped moving.

She wanted more—she pushed him further into memory. Two women in a small wooden house next to a river estuary were talking and then arguing. One was tall, one short, and the tall one grew rigid with anger.

"*¡Puta!*" shouted the tall one.

The short one smiled and bared a breast and offered it to the tall woman. The tall woman screamed.

Then even further into memory—the small woman with cinnamon skin and heavy breasts nursing a baby, singing to it as dawn overcame the night, and the woman smiled at the baby, a baby with skin lighter than her own. Then the face again, mutilated, now haloed in fire. And silence . . . And time . . .

She had been the woman who had reached out to the world with peeling black hands, even though she was dead.

She surged within Tata Victor, and he sat up as if he too felt the shock of realization. Then he collapsed with a thud to the floor.

She had had a body once . . . a woman's shapely body. Who had killed her when she was a woman? Who was the other woman in the vision? The spirit did not know how to go further into the past, and yet she was too restless to stop her quest.

The man rose again before she knew what to do. He tried to calm her, chanting and pulling her slowly out of his body, singing the words to lull her to his will.

The boy blew out the flames in the tapers.

THREE

CENTRAL PARK SPIRITS

*P*alo Monte is bush magic from the islands, and maybe Africa too, like they say. And maybe all those quaint customs, like killing chickens, and the use of all those words that start with "N"—*Nsambia, nkisi, nfuiri, nganga*—give it an air of authenticity. *Nsambia* just means "God above," but when you say it like that you can feel the bush in it, that *Nsambia* is lord of the bush, of the runaway indentured servants and slaves of the Caribbean past, of everything wild and free. But when you're from the city, you gotta make do with what's at hand. So Tata Victor and his kid mixed the skull and bones from the island with dirt from Central Park, and they put it all at the bottom of the cauldron.

"*Nfuiri nganga*, I am your master, for good and also for evil," said Victor.

Paleros ain't no joke. They see the world as a tapestry, and if there ain't no dark threads, there can't be any shining good ones either.

More authenticity: he pressed a knife blade into his forearm, and a small trickle of blood poured into the cauldron.

Now the *nfuiri* knew what she'd been thirsty for all along. She suckled on the salt and sugar in the blood, and grooved on Victor's words, relaxing, getting confident, being what she could be.

The flames in the tapers lighted and grew creepy huge, like shadows of tall witches with long nails.

The boy gasped. And for the first time since she'd woken into the world of the spirit, the *nfuiri* really understood what was behind human words: feeling and the will to know.

The boy cried, "She's lighting the flames on her own!" The kid was afraid of her, but his fear was almost like an attraction. And the *nfuiri*, she liked the attention.

A witch's cauldron, yeah. Thrice to mine and thrice to thine and all that. But it wasn't just a brew they were cooking up, they were making a whole 'nother being. Just without the body.

The ingredients were all meant to enhance the *nfuiri*'s faculties, to make her braver than brave, swift-moving, sharp of hearing and sight. Tata Victor placed on top of the skull the mummified body of a hunting spaniel, to help her track the victims. The boy added a piece of hollowed-out bamboo filled with mercury, and the barks of Ceiba, mahogany, pine, oak and other trees she had no clue about. The man put in dashes of red pepper, chili, garlic, ginger, onion, cinnamon and rue, and then added bucketfuls more of dirt. Then he made a hole in the dirt, and the kid poured in from different containers live insects: fire ants, red *gongoli* worms, termites. He put in a brown spider, a large mouse.

From another tank, the man let out into the cauldron a scorpion, and from a third he released a centipede with a bright orange segmented body. The centipede raised its little horns. The spider puffed up to double its size. And the *paleros* threw on dirt and quickly planted some long green stripling sticks.

Tata Victor Tumba Fuego and his boy buried her on a waxing moon night under a live oak tree in Central Park. They instructed her to roam and observe people, and not to worry, they'd be back.

Her hearing and smell, sharpened—that was the point of adding the dog to the brew.

She could hear the people in the park talking. They thought the park was just a place with nice green things growing.

Nfuiri gave a spirit chuckle. These humans had not a clue. They'd never bothered praying to the willows that hung over the Pool, nor the locust trees that lined the paths, the sycamores and oaks, the dawn redwoods in their lonely grove.

The trees were brooding, waiting for their time. But there were others beside the tree spirits. Unlike the *nkisis* and *nfuiris* in the cauldrons in Tata Victor's home, these didn't really know what they were.

She heard them murmuring:

"My mother pulled me out of her body under her long, bustled dress, and threw me into the Pool. I saw my little body float . . . I was glad that such a frail thing had died before it truly lived . . . I despised that small, helpless body. Sometimes if I see a child near the Pool, I give it a little push to see if it will fall in. Just a little push gives me the energy to flit and giggle. Most of the children don't notice, but one little girl felt my frozen baby fingers on her wrist and saw my face, pale as after I'd drowned. I yearned for the warmth in her body, and pulled her towards me. She screamed and screamed until her mother came. . . . "

"I'd run up the path from the Pool, past the Loch, to the Meer. I used to love to run. It was what made me feel alive. I was so caught up in running. I didn't hear them in time. They brought me down, and I tried to struggle, but one clamped his hand down on my mouth and another held my legs, while the third one pulled down my running pants and climbed on me. Later they tore me open like a bag. They left me under the trees near the Pool. I saw so much blue among the leaves of the weeping willow that I thought I was drowning in the sky as I died. . . . "

"We were sick and so poor we had to sleep in the park at night. They wouldn't let us stay in the workhouse after Fanny died because they thought we had caught the Spanish flu from her. That year so many died of the influenza, but in the city they blamed the poor for it. We had to come to the park uptown at 103rd Street to sleep, and the boy was crying for his mother. It was only November but that night it was unseasonably cold. I lay on top of my boy to cover him up. I could feel his warm heart, pulsing slowly like a little bird or a rabbit. I willed my warmth into

him . . . So I died smiling. I wish I knew what happened to my boy. That's why I roam. I know my boy didn't die in the park with me. I waited and roamed, but I never saw my little boy again. . . . "

The voices grew more insistent as the dark got deeper. But in the end she realized she couldn't do much for them.

The little world of her cauldron was in an uproar at first. The centipede snapped off two of the tarantula's hinged and hairy legs. Afterwards, the centipede curled around the mushy exoskeleton of the tarantula. Then a rock knocked the centipede's head downside. The scorpion that had been biding its time sank its stinger into the centipede's jaws.

Engorged by their venom, she rattled her invisible chains.

The man and the boy came back for her almost a month later, on a dark and moonless night. By then, *nfuiri* was hot with poison from the crawlers, and impatient to see the man again. When he dug up the cauldron, she shook the pot and helped to push it up out of the earth.

Tata Victor took a cloth from his jacket, wiped the dirt from the cauldron's sides.

"She's ready to work." He grinned at the boy.

He charged her with her first task. He told her that now she was a powerful *nfuiri* that could track like a dog, coil around prey like a centipede and sting like a scorpion. She could fly like a wasp, roil like red ants, claw, sniff, see, hear, touch, heal, kill, hurtle through the air, conjure up the wanderer, speak to the dead. She would not be just a voice crying voiceless in the night.

He asked her to twist like wire around the womanlike willow that grew by the pool until she had squeezed it dry of life.

She crawled up the willow bark like a fast moving moldering kiss and when she reached the tender buds at the top branches, they fell off all at once.

The night before Tata Victor came back, a man attacked a woman at nightfall under the dead willow. He sliced off her dress with a knife and penetrated her like a pack dog until she cried out so piteously the *nfuiri* could not bear her cries.

"*A woman such as I was, a woman alone and followed,*" said one of the wispy voices.

"*Save her then, if she is like you,*" said the spirit of the drowned baby.

"*I could not save myself,*" said the running girl. "*I do not know how to help her. Why should I save her? I did not know how to save myself.*"

"*I will help her,*" said the *nfuiri* from atop her tree.

"*You did not die here,*" said the spirit of the running girl.

"*But I have grown into something different in this park. Different from what I was,*" she pointed out, real friendly-like. "*I am an* nfuiri, *and I am more powerful than you. I am known by humans.*"

"*How so?*"

"*I can do.*"

"*What is 'do'?*" said the spirit of the baby.

"*To do is one of the things that makes a human,*" said the nfuiri.

"*That is not so. Spirits cannot do as humans do.*"

"*I can make humans feel me.*"

"*You did not die here. How can you haunt this place? You were only brought here. Your death was not marked by this place.*"

"*She did not die here. She cannot stay in this park. She is not one of us.*"

"*You should not be here,*" said the running girl's spirit.

"*You must leave this place,*" said the spirit of the baby.

"*I cannot leave until my master bids me. It is by his will that I do as humans do.*"

"*Spirits cannot have human masters! How can that be possible?*" one cried, and they began to argue among themselves.

She shut out their cries. She could not directly help the woman, and because she was as pissed as an *nfuiri* could be, she started to rock the willow back and forth, back and forth, back and forth, until all its roots loosened and broke. The shaking of the tree made the woman scream but the sound of disaster only made the man thrust harder. The tree fell on the couple, crushing the man's skull and killing him instantly.

The woman was trapped too, but not hurt. She screamed through the night, and was still whimpering when she was rescued in the morning by one of the park's keepers. She told them that she had been running in the park, and the man had pinned her down and raped her. And then a ghost had made the tree crush her attacker.

At this point the *nfuiri* knew that one other human besides Tata Victor . . . had felt her strength. The *nfuiri* was intrigued. She knew she was bound to Tata Victor, but now she was interested in a life beyond his control.

When Tata Victor and the boy came back on the night of the full moon, she saw a shadow following them. She was free and yet not free at all. She saw the shadow's eyes watching like two deeper pits of night within the night. Guess who?

Nfuiri struck Tata Victor down. He belted out a laugh, because this was an exciting game to him. He opened his arms, and knelt down next to the fallen trunk, touching and testing, even as his eyes rolled up in his head. Genio watched with mouth open.

Those other eyes watched from the shadows.

In Tata Victor's presence, the *nfuiri* couldn't will herself to find the owner of those eyes. Tata Victor tried to cradle the *nfuiri*, fling her back and forth as he'd done when he'd found her in the forest on the island. But she had more power now. He was still master of the cauldron. But under the stars fanning the darkness over the trees, she made him cry out.

"What?" He knelt on the grass. "What do you want?" He softened then, and she pressed him.

"She was a rich man's mistress. I mean, you were a rich man's mistress," said Tata Victor. "And you were killed out of jealousy." He shook his head and breathed deeply, as if trying to see more. "You only wanted to be a mother to your child."

She released him and he fell forward, eating grass and dirt.

And then she looked for those other eyes, but they were gone.

FOUR

STEPPING IN AND OUT

The dreaded cutting passed in the blink of an eye. All of a sudden it was: been there, done that. I got down with the after-feeling of leeches yumming on my back, and the burning in my thumbs. I even started losing my taste for badass strutting and the slapping off of folks who bumped into me on the street. I was ready to fly with the *nfuiri*.

Victor was sitting at his table in the reading room next to the window, and I was sitting opposite him. "For your first outing," he said, "I want you to stay close to my place, and to choose an easy target, somebody who could use a little *nfuiri* guidance, so to speak, but nobody you know real good."

"Damn," I said. "I know a few people who could use fixing by an *nfuiri*."

"Not for your first time," snapped Victor. "I got an easier target: them thugs that sit on the front steps."

"Okay," I shrugged. And then a thought came to me. "They deal even in daylight. Could use some shaking up."

"What's worse is that they piss against the walls outside the window at night," he growled. "And not one of them took notice of who might have come round the day Genio died."

At midnight of the second day, after the ritual chants, and under Victor's direction, I took a long draught from a bottle of Wray and Nephew's rum, and spewed it all out onto the cauldron. Marking her with my spit, so to speak, very important in *nfuiri* endeavors.

Victor lit a cigar for me, and I took a deep drag.

"Go in, talk to her and go on in."

I looked at the cauldron, and studied the little green saplings growing out of it. Then the dirt, underneath; then I tried to see the world inside the cauldron as Victor had taught me: the soft herbs of peace, the venom of battle, the sun in white rocks, the moon in black meteorite, the ocean from water, the star bursts from the cigar. I blew tobacco out. I went into the rot, the earth, the deep stink of death, the spirit fluttering. I felt her heat. I saw her dreams of fire, her travels through the forest, the charred hands, her yearning for water.

Now, I saw Tata Victor lifting up a woman from the floor. The massive body, the snake-like hair, the open eyes looking up at me, as transfixed as I was looking down at her. At me. It was my body, eyes rolled up into the head, arms stretched out on the floor, a smile playing on my lips.

Now I was stepping on out with the *nfuiri*, wafting out the window.

In the street, we floated carelessly over the tops of the buildings, and then I pushed the *nfuiri* higher, high as she would take me. If this killed me, then I would die appeased, I would become what I always told people they could be: a part of every fucking thing in this world.

What a fucking trip! The trip of my life!

I flew over sooty rooftops, ate and rushed with blue night wind, saw hundreds of mice swarming in the scrub between buildings and with the *nfuiri* I scavenged like the mice. I got all tangled up in the top branches of a skinny oak tree, daring itself out of the sidewalk. I felt like I was the oak throwing up arms to catch at the *nfuiri*.

Seen from above, the boys in their do-rags made me feel as playful as the mice. I saw the thug who'd pushed me on the day I found out about Genio. I saw for the first time that the kid had striking green eyes. He was, despite his large jaw and a keloid as thick as a finger on his forehead, just a beautiful boy. A gun butt jutted from between Beauty's T-shirt and his baggy jeans. The other boy was nondescript except for his black jacket with red lettering on the back that spelled "Park East."

The boys sold *perico*, mostly to dudes in cars that slowed down as they approached the corner.

Beauty walked back and forth between the corner and a building next to Victor's, and *nfuiri* and I followed him. When he had almost reached the corner a second time, we pulled down his pants with one strong jerk.

The boy reached for his gun with one hand, touched his crotch, then his pants. He pulled the whole gun out and whipped around.

"Whosit?"

We slapped the gun out of his hands and pulled it through the air before letting it drop. Beauty turned and his eyes bugged when he saw the gun just floating there. This was the shit!

The gun fired. Beauty tried to take off, but not before we ransacked his pockets and dangled his packets in the air like a string of fat stars. Then he collapsed in a trash can.

But my clean-up work wasn't done.

We floated over to the corner. Beauty climbed out of the trash can and tried to say something to the other boy but choked on his words. Then he took a quick breath. "The stuff flew in the air, bro. It . . . it flew away from me. And the gun did, too." He took off the tight black head rag. "I know it sounds like it ain't true, but I swear to God, Chulo, it's true."

"You need to stop taking lines when we work, man."

"I didn't! You don't understand. It was out of nowhere. It was like a *fantasma*, man. Like maybe that guy that got killed last week . . . like maybe he did it."

"What you saying, fool? Where your gun at?"

"The *fantasma* took it!"

"There ain't no *fantasma*, man. That shit don't exist!"

A car stopped, and a white man with coarse grey hair leaned out of the window and held out what looked like a few hundred green smackers in his hand.

Beauty handed over the last of his foil packets. Before the man could take it, we swatted it away.

"Hey, what was that?" said the man.

Beauty reached down to pick up the packet from the street, but I exerted more pressure, and *nfuiri* flicked it in the air and started playing ping-pong with it.

"You playing with me, boy?" said the man in the car, iron in his voice.

We flipped, kicked and punted the packet every time the boy tried to pick it up, until we had him on the far corner beyond the lights flashing slowly from green to red to yellow. The light was red when we dove into the sewer and then reached back out with a watery arm and sucked down the last packet.

The light turned green and the car crossed to the opposite corner. The man with silver hair got out. His eyes were the color of ice. He was holding a gun, and his hand was trembling.

"Boy, where's my stuff?"

"Mister, I'm sorry, I don't know what happened. Chulo will go get more. . . . "

"There ain't no more," said Chulo.

The man raised the gun.

"Oh, shit," muttered Beauty.

We batted the gun slightly and the heavy metal ball that would have opened a funneling wound in the boy's chest ricocheted off the car bumper and into the bricks of the building right on the corner.

Lights went on in a couple of buildings on Lexington, and old Beauty threw the money back at the man.

The man reeled and looked around wildly, as if he thought the person who had pulled at his gun would be within shooting distance. Then he got into the car and sped off.

"What I'd tell you?" said Beauty.

The other boy shook his head. "You was high and he was maddog."

"I didn't do the shit! You know I don't do the shit when I'm working."

"We owe Malo money, now. Whatchu goin' to do 'bout that."

Still ghetto even in my flight, I suddenly bumped hard into Chulo. He almost fell, but the *nfuiri* held out an invisible mesh and prevented him from banging his head on the concrete.

"What the fuck?"

"It's the *fantasma*," said Beauty, backing away.

"Stop that crazy talk. There ain't no . . . "

I pulled at Chulo's pants, started to tear at them, jerking until they were down at his ankles and then I pulled down his white underpants.

"*Ay, ay, ay,*" said Chulo and I grabbed at his thighs.

Then he laughed. I slapped him a few times on his bare bottom. He tried to run and tripped over his pants, fell to the ground right on the bones of his hand and howled.

"Help me, Beto, please! Is a ghost or something, you wasn't shitting. Les get outta here!"

"Man, this shit ain't worth it," said Beauty. He grabbed Chulo and helped him get up. Beauty's forehead was so creased he looked like an old man.

"I'm going back to McDonald's. I don't want no *fantasma* snatching me to hell!"

FIVE
HEADMASTER

I woke in a sweat to the sound of rain like a firing squad on the zinc roof and a smell of Florida water somewhere.

He took my hand and said the hurricane would pass. "Remember the life-death plant by the river, when you kiss it, it goes to sleep?" His voice soothed me and I relaxed. "Fill the *bóveda* glasses for me, *nena*. So I'm always with you."

There was a wet towel soaked in Florida water on my forehead.

"Papi?"

"Damn, do I look that old?" said Victor. His beetle brow smoothed out. I was in a small room with just a bed in it and a dresser. The sanctum sanctorum.

"How you feeling?"

"I gotta admit—faint."

He nodded. I remembered the street, the boys, the exhilaration of swirling in the air and watching normally empty eyes start to wonder about shit for the first time, and I smiled.

Victor smiled back.

"I want to go back."

"You need to rest up. And then there's more I need to show you."

"I want to know about mounting."

"Right now, you should eat something."

The wind. Out there the blue wind was part of me, my body was just like a compass left behind. I was the night wind and her, of course, the *nfuiri*.

My eyelids fluttered. My body felt heavy, but deep down in me was that long reeling expanse of blue.

"I'm not hungry. The night is still in me."

Victor sat on the bed, which made a thwacking sound. "Finish it, then, but you know you can't mount. Not yet, anyway."

In the morning, Abuela said she had made him go. "He was a devil worshipper."

She was a tiny skinny thing with yellow eyes and hundreds of freckles on her wrinkled skin. When I looked at her, I couldn't help thinking of the island saying that yellow eyes were liar's eyes.

"No!" I screamed at her. "No." Papi didn't worship devils. "Trees, water!" I babbled at her. I was little and couldn't really say the important things I thought I knew: Papi practiced a different religion, not a bad one; and Abuela insisted on saying that Papi worshipped devils, when it was Abuela who believed in devils, not Papi.

Abuela knelt before her little blue robed statue of Mary on the night table. "Blessed Mary, save this child from the devils her father worshipped. Mother of light, fight the darkness in her."

I wanted the spirits of water and trees to love me. I didn't want Mary to take me away from them, so I threw the statue at the wall.

Just the head broke off, and Abuela went over to grab it. "¡Mala!" she yelled. "¡Bruja!"

And it was about then that I fell down.

When I finally got over the dengue, weeks later, I accepted that Andrés Mata, my papi, had gone to El Bronx.

Abuela tried to make nice. She conceded that I wasn't really "mala." It was the dengue.

I came to New York, and looked for traces of him all over the five boroughs, but I never found him. I became the bruja Abuela said I was.

That last night. The life-death plant, his gentle hands, the love in his voice—he was the only one who had really loved me—the sound of river water. And now: the East River, the trees. The Grand Concourse, the black rooftops that had never looked so wonderful, the long-ass and wide streets, the wailing sirens, the people scurrying like ants . . .

The eyes.

Where was Andrés Mata?

The eyes in the man-made forest.

My father? I need to know . . .

A sudden flash of a man's body in a rundown mess that could have been a ghetto apartment anywhere . . .

It could have been any dark-haired man's body lying on the floor like that.

No, not him. Please, not him.

Her child. *Nfuiri* needed to know about the child.

Shit, how do you even argue with a spirit? Since I didn't know how, I did what I usually do. I tried to hit her, but of course there was nobody to hit. Worse, I didn't have anything to hit with. It was just the ghetto energy, without the ghetto girl, and I was dealing with an energy wilder than any ghetto girl's.

And talk about a sudden fear of heights . . .

The woman's big fat body, the eyes opened wide, the hands that shot up in the air, Victor starting up his chants, cradling the big woman against the freefall into a wall.

When I woke up, my whole body ached, my head pounded with what seemed like migraines at different points all over, and I could hardly speak, my throat hurt so much.

"You need to talk to the *nfuiri nganga*. Asperge with rum and your saliva, feed her rooster blood and honey, but talk to her. Smoke your cigar and talk to her. You tell her what you want, but when she talks to you, you have to listen, too."

"Ah din no she have enting to aay . . . " I croaked.

Hours later, I was sitting up in Victor's bed. He had pouchy bags under his eyes. I think he looked so tired because he had had to sleep on the sofa, which he didn't really fit on. He had made me some kind of Cuban stew, which had strange yellow and purple root vegetables in it.

They didn't taste any different than the gray and white tubers Ricans cook with, which I don't like either. "Mmm, interesting tubers," I muttered.

"The *nfuiri nganga* gives you her ears, she gives you flight, above all and beyond she gives you the gift of vision. She ain't just some slave. She's ascending in the spiritual hierarchy. She's an *nfuiri* because what killed her didn't just kill her body. She's striving for completion, too. When she directs you towards something, you have to let her go in that direction."

"She wants her child. Something about eyes."

Victor stood still, stared at me for what seemed an endless beat before he blinked. "You know who the child is?"

"That girl that looks like a demon version of Betty Boop? I know that she came to see you. I ran into her." Now I gave him my own "what the hell" stare.

Victor nodded a little too placidly. "Jahaira, the girl's aunt, was in my *munanso* for a while. She led me to the bones."

"How did Jahaira know about the bones?"

"She found them. The body was buried in a dress she recognized from her sister, near the house they lived in. It had been buried near the house. But she didn't report it."

I thought of Chico's story about going to see Aurora that last time.

"The zinc-roofed shack?"

"How'd you know about that?"

"Out in the countryside in PR, people live in these tiny zinc-roofed shacks. Or they used to. I lived in one."

Victor nodded. "My family in Cuba lived in a house with a palm roof. A zinc roof would have been a luxury."

"Okay, so you win the poverty contest."

His eyebrows went up and down like Groucho Marx's. "What's the matter, Fina?"

I thought of Aurora and her cloud of gold-kinked hair. She had basically rejected Chico, or that's the way he told it. But he had rejected her too, thrown her over for Isis. Hadn't seemed like homeboy was mad at her. But she'd been real mad at him. Who could blame her? He was fucking Miss Universe when his baby was in the hospital.

And this Aurora of the pretty hair, this was the *nfuiri* in my cauldron? She was the spirit that was freeing up my body, which is really what I had been hoping Chico would do. But in a very different way.

"Tata, I want to use the bones to find out about Genio. I don't want to go running into the girl and not knowing how to use the bones. I know I can find her, or whoever killed Genio. When you really gonna teach me how to use these bones?"

Tata Victor's nostrils flared, he got the red glow in his eyes of a demon from a horror movie, or of someone in one of those old one-shot polaroids from the eighties.

"I have many *muertos*," he said, narrowing his eyes. "I have the Ancient One, and we both know what the Ancient One can do. I don't need to learn anything from you . . . "

"I wasn't meaning no disrespect . . . "

"I want my boy, Fina. I miss my boy. He was a good boy." Victor sat down, and he looked away.

"I know." I got up from the bed, feeling suddenly real wobbly. I hugged him and felt his shoulder blades under his black T-shirt. Then he put his arms around me, and his lips were coming on top of my lips and I could smell tobacco and coffee on him, smells which were so familiar that I really wanted to close my eyes and keep on kissing him.

He was the one who pulled back and rubbed his eyes. "I'm sorry, Fina."

"Tata, what I need from you now is kind of different, don't you agree?"

He looked at me and bowed his head slightly and this time when he looked away, he sank back into the space of grief and didn't hear anything I said about how I was going home now, and would call him later. He didn't notice when I left the room, or even when I pressed the button lock on the side of the door to his apartment and closed the door. He was perfectly still, absent now from real time, and I hoped closer to Genio in his silence and solitude.

Later on that night when I called his apartment, the phone just rang and rang, and I knew he was still sitting there in the dark, eyes closed, waiting patiently for the moment when his silence and the boy's would meet.

I called in sick to work every day for the next week.

When I entered the copy room a week or so later, and saw the two Xerox machines piled with boxes of crap that I was meant to copy, my feeling of being out of sync was complete. Like, here I was—somebody who could ride the night—working in a fucking copy room.

Bill, my quasi-boss, a blonde guy with the whitest teeth that made him look like the sunshine kid, walked out of his office. Bill spent his summers traveling in Patagonia and Australia, and his traveler side was what he was proud of, not his job as Master of the Duplicating Room.

"What's up, Bill?"

"Well, ah Fina, you know, I don't know what to say."

I tipped my head one way, and my extensions clicked and clacked. "What?"

It turned out that Beltoff had been keeping tabs on me. And since I'd barely been working there for a few months, and had missed a week or so of work lately, he was firing me.

"But I was sick."

"I know," said Bill. A sunflash of teeth. "But you were out a week and a half, and you couldn't provide a doctor's note. You know how the headmaster is." He nodded, looking away. "You know."

I nodded.

I didn't really have to gather my things, because I didn't keep a lot of shit in the copy room. Besides, I suddenly had a good idea. I was going home, to smoke a cigar with the lit end in my mouth, mix spit with rum and talk talk talk to my *nfuiri*.

I walked by the Headmaster's office and asked the two boys who sometimes sat at the front desks how long Beltoff would be in his office today. One of them didn't answer, and the other, a tall boy with huge gray eyes and windswept hair, said "'Til 5 pm."

I walked past them and down the hallway. I looked in quickly. Beltoff sat at his desk. He was wearing an Armani-looking suit that would have looked dazzling on any of the other men in my life. On him it looked like sausage casing.

I ducked out before he looked up.

I went to Lori Shellman's office and caught her just as she was on her way out, closing the door behind her. The olive green pantsuit she had on made her look kind of distinguished.

She looked at me and frowned. "You look different. Did you lose weight?"

"I found something better than Italian food. But that ain't why I'm here."

She kept her gaze fixed on me and nodded several times. "You know, I heard Beltoff fired you. Bill told me. If only . . . "

"Girl, you know what you wanted from me? I decided I can do it."

"Really? But it's kind of late for that now. I mean for you."

"It doesn't matter. Just let me use your office. I gotta do shit to make this work. I can't have nobody seeing what I'm doing."

At about 4:00 pm, I tapped my left foot three times and muttered, " *Nchile bakiakuantala bakongo.*" Then I sat down at

Lori Shellman's cluttered desk, and faced a little blackboard on the wall above it.

I called to my mind Beltoff sitting at his desk, reading over a letter.

His suit. It wasn't just a brown suit. It was a tapestry of silvery gray and deep rich brown. Intricate wavy lines and dots. It smelled as rich as it looked. The little collar of the silk shirt under it wasn't blue, it was fucking *azure*. Under the shirt was his pink neck.

With breath we started drawing the most basic pattern of the *munanso*. The sign of roads meeting. The sign of the cross.

My eyes were shut and I was a few hundred feet away from him, but in my mind I saw Beltoff slapping his neck. To him it must have felt like an invisible long-nailed finger was furrowing a line down his neck and then across it.

The large circle of the world in the middle, the small circles of the other worlds at each corner of the cross.

"Now, what is that?" Beltoff got up from his chair, but *nfuiri* had already started to twine up his leg.

He was swatting at the air, but when *nfuiri* grabbed his waist, he couldn't help but push his pelvis forward. And when she started to shoot tendrils of energy up past his ears, I started to really see him.

I was fucking surprised. He wasn't thinking about Shellman. And I was barely a blip in his brain. It was the name tags that worried him. A special function for the chairman of the board of trustees was starting at 6 pm in the school's Great Hall. He was worried that there might be a mix-up in the name tags.

And what about the toilet paper in the bathrooms next to the Great Hall? He'd ordered restocking yesterday, and twice today, but what if there wasn't any toilet paper?

In Lori Shellman's office, I grinned, even as my eyeballs rolled up in my head.

Quickly I made *nfuiri* vine around his waist I shot my energy into his arms and he danced.

With his own hands as clumsy, heavy tools, we tore open the lovely azure shirt. We did it so forcefully that two of the buttons popped off.

He started to rub himself against a wall. The coldness made him laugh aloud.

There was a knock on the door. It was the sensitive kid with the windswept hair. Beltoff smiled; he liked the kid's pretty face. Even more than he admired the kid's looks, he envied the boy's honesty.

"How come you're not wearing your shirt, sir?"

"Why don't you come in, Michael?"

"I'm on my way home."

"Michael, you have such nice hair." Beltoff put his fingers in the boy's hair. The silky texture made his hand tremble.

The boy pulled away.

We pressed him. He had always wanted to do this. Not just with Michael but with a few others who passed through his offices at the Balder School.

"Michael, if you please let me please you, I can solve your tuition problems, and please you even more."

Beltoff went down on his knees and started to rub his head at the boy's crotch. The boy bit his lip.

"You'll pay for my tuition?" The boy's eyes hooded over. He had one semester left at the school, but his parents were divorcing, and he wasn't sure whether he could stay for his last semester.

"I'll put you on a scholarship for the semester, and even give you pocket money."

"Tuition's enough!" The boy took off his belt, and started to unzip his gray Levis.

Beltoff snuffled in there, and he was pleasantly surprised.

Beltoff took Michael into his mouth, and the thoughts he had again were a fucking surprise to me.

Hiram thought of Jerry Davis, a boy he'd loved deeply when he was a boy. But he'd also made fun of Jerry. Along with all the other boys, he'd called Jerry pansy, girlie and fag. Jerry Davis had ended up in and out of hospital wards throughout the years.

Now he was going to cure Jerry, heal him, bring him on out.

When he was done with his healing, he turned his head and saw Lori Shellman and three other teachers standing in the doorway.

SIX
YELLOW EYES

She gives you her vision
She ain't just some slave
She wants you to hear
What she has to say . . .
Born in a forest
Died in a river
Nfuiri *of air*
Come back forever . . .

There was more to it, a whole long chant in a sandy voice like Tata Victor's. In my dream the words seemed to write themselves on what looked like yellowed parchment, but that was all I remembered when I woke up.

I rushed to find paper and pen and wrote down the lines I remembered. Then I made coffee and sat down at the kitchen table.

But that chocolate bitter taste didn't work for me now. I felt even more sleepy. I looked in the fridge, but wasn't hungry either. That was weird, because usually I plan my meals and snacks right at the beginning of the day. I love food. I love noshing on everything from Twix bars to steak roulade. But I just wasn't hungry.

When I looked in the mirror, I was real surprised. I looked kind of . . . well, wan . . . a word I associate with tall thin David Bowie types. Or characters in old poetry.

There I was in that mirror with my Medusa-like extensions floating over my ashy face.

It was only when I looked at her, I mean, at the cauldron, that I felt better. The *palos* looked taller and seemed to be pulsing slightly, as if calling out to me, so I went for my Wray and Nephews rum and the cigars.

Even before I started to sprinkle *chamba* water, I thought that I wanted to be the night again, the trees, the bright falling air. And I thought of Isis. I looked for her in the way I was learning. I closed my eyes and looked for her, and sent the *nfuiri* looking, too. Looking for and at her. First at her hazel eyes, the upward tilt to her nose . . . her kinkiness that wasn't so different from mine.

Walking, she was walking. Her hair was really wavy today. She had on some sort of greenish voile blouse, and this dusky afternoon as she walked east to west through the park, her eyes turned yellow in the refracted sunlight. A smile playing on her lips.

Chico? They'd spent the previous night apart, and the whole day, and she would see him soon, and the more she thought of how soon it would be, the more the smile caught her whole face.

Night started its fainting fall, and the lamps glowed like a line of well-matched moons.

A short man walked by, giving her the once-over, and she pulled her back straighter. The man pursed his lips into a pseudo kiss. These Nuyoricans from the ghetto! She never went to public places like this on the island. After she'd seen the dead bird pulsing with ants, she never wanted to go to parks in Puerto Rico, filled with pigeons and their vile infestations. But lately she was attracted to the park. She didn't know why.

Look, there was that fat woman with the poodle. She had noticed her the day of her birthday party. Ridiculous! These New Yorkers were too much. That woman's entire sense of culture, condensed into the curly haired little dog. These Nuyoricans thought the Puerto Rican Day parade was culture! Well, rice and beans did not a culture make! She wondered what that fat woman in her sky-high shorts tripping over her absurd poodle would think if she told her that?

And then she felt a turn, was she going to throw up? She stopped walking, and held herself very carefully, as if she was balancing a crystal vase on top of her head. Or was it her head itself that felt as transparent as crystal? It was like someone was seeing into her head. She covered her face with her hands.

We passed a skinny guy with a moustache, kind of dorky looking. But Isis tried to catch his eye. And she did. The dork's beady little eyes started eating her up at the eyes, darted to her breasts and then traveled down to her bare legs. She pretended she was displeased, but fuck, she wanted anybody, even the dork, to look at her. She tipped her nose into the air and rushed past him.

The *nfuiri* was even more interested than I in this fucked up behavior. She pressed hard until Isis started growing aware that there were, as it were, other eyes. She stopped just a few feet away from the footbridge and swayed slightly in the afternoon breeze, covering her face with her hands.

A man, an older man with white hair, walked towards her from the footbridge, and asked her if she was all right.

"I just felt something strange," she said.

What she felt was the way we were trying to see. To see through her yellow eyes.

Nfuiri needed to scan the long stretch of her memory to find the broken past.

I, on the other hand, was cool with the fact that physically I was a mile away from the park. I could taste the breeze through the elms, the hemlocks and the empress trees, soaking up sun warmth, feeling what it was like to be something I had never been—a beautiful woman.

The man nodded. "Strange things have been happening in the park lately."

"Strange? How?" She broke into a sweat. She itched to run her hands over her body, and squeeze the tips of her breasts, her belly as warm as a rabbit, the hungry opening between her legs. And she was terrified that she was feeling this way in public in front of some vulgar person she didn't know.

I didn't know how far I wanted to go, but the *nfuiri* did. Isis found herself suddenly tortured by the desire to bite the old man. That had to be the *nfuiri*. Because the old man seemed a little dried up to me, like he would taste real bad, like moldy bread.

"Not a bad thing, actually," the old man said. "A rapist got killed, or hurt. The victim said there was a demon in the park that helped her. I just say that's not a very nice way of describing the homeless." The old man smirked.

"Oh, I see." Isis looked away.

"Are you sure you're okay?" said the old man. "You seem to be out of breath."

She didn't answer.

Finally, the old man continued on his way through the park.

She slowly breathed in air that was green and red, the freshness of grass on clayey rock. I noticed through her eyes, as though for the first time, the beauty of the park, how each leaf on each tree refracted light, all changing and transforming momentarily with the light from gold to green to brown dazzling my eyes.

As we approached the footbridge, she put a hand out to steady herself on the rough-hewn wooden railing, and the *nfuiri* enjoyed the unaccustomed tingling caused by the rough surface of the bark.

Isis pressed her pelvis into the railing. Through her clothes she could feel each burl and crevice in the wood, as if she was naked. From over the wooden railing, she stared at the water, frothing icily over the stones in one spot, and a tranquil green in another. It was as if she had never before seen these little pools that she passed by in the park on her way to Chico's. The water had an unforeseen depth.

She thought now that she saw a woman's shape in the tranquil part of the water. Like a shadow in the water, a shadow with rounded breasts and hips, extending its arms, reaching outward for her, reaching up.

No, that was impossible. It was because she was lightheaded. She had that sensation that people could see into her brain, could see her thoughts, so she kept her face in her hands as she tried to figure out whether it was just some sort of sand ridge there in the water, or a series of rocks, maybe, that looked like a woman's body.

But through her eyes refracted through the *nfuiri*, I could see it there, hovering clearly, a deep shadow in the water shaped like a woman.

She closed her eyes.

The small woman with generous breasts and hips and wild brown hair, frizzed gold at the tips by sun and wind. This woman was standing next to a man, a man with pale skin and black hair. The dark-skinned woman was wearing a simple white dress, almost like a slip, and no clothes underneath. The man was looking down at her, letting his hand slide down her backside. The woman took the man's other hand and pressed it to her crotch. That slut, that slut her husband had loved.

The *nfuiri* saw in her, beyond her. The two women were standing on a sandy beach at the point where a river delta joined the ocean. The small woman was round in the hips and the breasts, more voluptuous than even the tall woman with the yellow eyes, who was staring at the smaller woman with hatred.

The small woman opened her mouth and a string of the most delicious and obscene barbarities spilled out.

"*Cállate ya, cállate ya,*" said the tall woman.

She felt hollowed out, and irritated by a dog's shrill yelps.

"*Cállate ya, perrito. Cállate,*" Isis said to the poodle in a pink suede collar who had awakened her from her reverie. The images and details in her mind started to blur.

When it heard her voice, so gentle and loving, despite the fact that she was telling it to shut up, it started wagging its tail, and tried to jump out of its owner's grasp.

"*Cállate, perrito ridículo*," Isis whispered, and started laughing. She wanted to touch that dog.

"Whachu saying to my dog?"

"Oh, nothing," said Isis to the big woman. "Just telling it that everything is all right."

"Sounded like you was telling it to shut up."

"To hush, that's what people say here, no? To tell children to stop crying. I meant to tell it to hush."

Isis put out a hand to touch the dog. And it was because of the *nfuiri* that all at once we felt the dog's coat, its delicate bones, the wobble of its organs, the blood pumping throughout its body.

Isis drew back her hand. But really, she wanted to feel more, to feel the creature's heart in its body.

The dog's owner turned, and Isis accidentally touched the woman's face.

"Yo! You be careful with little Cleopachra. She is de-li-cat-a." The woman patted the dog. "Like glass." Her nostrils flared.

"Cleo . . . ?" Isis was tense. She wanted to shake the sensation inside of her, as clear as nausea, the ache to feel the world, to take it all up inside her. But I . . . I was syncing with the *nfuiri*, learning to hold the horse in place.

"Cleopatra, like the queen of Egypt?" Isis said, her gaze running over the woman: straightened hair, dyed blonde, tortured into a ponytail at the top of her head; body clad in a rag on top; and short pants that revealed all the stars and craters in her flesh.

Isis was repelled by this woman. She hated her dog, too.

"It's Cleopatra, with a T, you know," said Isis, finally. Then, impelled by the *nfuiri*, she added, "I'm sure you could care less about the pronunciation. What was it you called the poor little dog?"

And yet the dog and the woman throbbed with vital heat.

I started to see what the *nfuiri* wanted to do, and this time, I liked it, I really liked it.

The woman got agitated. She took her hand from the dog's coat and put it on her hip. "That's what I said, bitch. Cleopachra! Dinchu hear me?"

Isis suddenly knew what she wanted, and the thrill of knowing what she wanted, when most of the time she was torn by at least two, if not more, opposite feelings, filled her with relief.

Nfuiri pushed her to the logical conclusion.

Knowing that the violence would help me free myself of Isis, I went along with it. Isis put her hands on the dog's fluffy coat. We became aware of the fragility of the body that breathed beneath her fingertips, of the dumb little face that licked her hand. Then with both hands, as if she were opening a jar, she deftly broke the creature's neck. It sounded like the click of a lock.

The fat woman was dumbstruck. For a moment her mouth was a perfect circle.

Isis still wanted to scratch out the other's eyes, but I pushed her past that. She ran towards the line of lamps, which gleamed like moons, as if another world lay beyond.

The woman cried out, and then we mounted her. People gathered round her, among them the old man with white hair, a teenage girl wearing ripstop pants and a black man in plaid long shorts.

Her mouth trembling, the bereaved woman stretched out her arms and offered the dog to the gawkers.

The woman did not resist us at all. She thought what was riding her was part of what she was feeling, the panicked need to run to where the willow tree had died and throw the dead dog there, to bend down in the cold grass and slowly tear her hair out of her head by the roots so the growing pain in her body could match her heartache.

With both hands she tore out the thick strands on top of her head, the difficult hair that she'd straightened only that morning. She barely felt the pain, as if she was pulling feathers out of a chicken, the way her grandmother used to do. The blood from the top of her head streamed into her mouth.

We lifted up the heavy sack of a woman, and rode her out of the park in the same direction that Isis had run.

Nfuiri knew now who Isis was. The woman on the bank of the river. The jealous woman. In the darkness that was her memory, the yellow eyes shone and started to throw out streams and pathways of light everywhere.

SEVEN
LOVE MIGRATES

It was after we tripped up, and tripped in, that old Isis, started to get cranky.

"Uh huh," you say, real careful like. Maybe you roll your eyes a little. Okay, sure, we can consider the question of whether the *nfuiri* was some excuse of mine for doing and seeing weird shit, or a symbol, like Lori Shellman said, a symbol of the part of me that liked to do and see weird shit.

Whatever she was, she was starting to get a little cranky. She kept pushing images into my brain of Isis' eyes with that yellow Central Park lamps glow in them. She wanted to try out more of her *nfuiri* powers, but I was tired.

I didn't want to step in again so soon after the Central Park experiment. I wanted to lie down. It's fucking exhausting to inhabit other people and make them tear out their hair or see faces, places and other shit they've spent a lot of time and maybe money trying to forget.

So the *nfuiri* was throwing plates around the apartment. They were breaking everywhere. I didn't care much about the plates—they were from the 99-cent store—but it was making a hell of a noise. And when somebody knocked on the door at some point, I was almost relieved, because I thought that would make her stop.

"Fina."

I stood silently a few feet from the door.

"Fina, are you okay?"

He sounded like he really was worried, so I went to the door, but I didn't open it.

"Fina, I can tell you're there. Please open the door."

A dish sailed past me, and I screamed "*¡Ay ay ay!*"—which says a lot about how upset I was, since I barely use my Spanish. Having spent formative years in the mean streets of Spanish Harlem, and even more formative years in the neurotic streets of the Upper West Side, I really wasn't an "*Ay ay ay*" type.

I finally opened the door. He was running a hand over a sexy day's-growth of beard. His look of hysterical concern really tore me up. I wanted to jump him right there.

"You're thin, Fina. You look thin and tired."

Shit, isn't it almost like a guy is making a pass when he tells you you're thin? Sure I was thinner than my usual 200 lbs, but thin?

I wanted to tell him he wasn't thin, he was juicy and sweet like a mango and I wanted to chomp on him. Instead I mealy-mouthed, "It's not a good time, *mijo*."

"Fina, I know there's something wrong. Look at your press-ons! Your nails are broken!"

I was fucking startled and looked down at my nails. There were black lines of dirt under some of them. Homeboy was right, I was a freak about my nails. But I hadn't even noticed. And then I ran my tongue over my lips and suddenly realized with horror that they were cracked.

"These weren't press-ons," I said weakly. "But I'm on my way to the beauty shop to get them touched up."

"I have a gig late tonight. Isis will be there. I have passes. Come?"

I couldn't really be worrying about my own physical reactions, after all. Inside, I was like a dam against Niagara, holding her from stepping out, from knocking my head against his and from punching him in the neck and sucking up his mouth with mine. She was starting to remember him, too.

I cackled deliriously.

"See you then," he said. His happy bounce up the steps really got to me.

So, okay, well, why not let her step on out? And step in. It was Isis she wanted after all.

I was late. Twenty dudes in white single-breasted suits stood on a raised platform. Round pink lights shone down on them. A blonde crooned into a contraption, and her voice seemed filled with static, noise-making that she loved her man.

I shoved my way through the crowd and finally spotted Isis sitting at a table next to the railing that separated the stage from the tables. She was pretending she didn't want to talk to a tall black guy.

I waved both arms in the air, and my jacket rose over my saggy stomach. The people standing near drew back.

Oh, God, that feeling like a light was turned on in my brain, and I couldn't turn it off. But damn if I was going to let it bonfire my brain.

"Hope you're not trying to hit on my sis?" I said to the black dude.

"Nah, just trying to get a seat." My mean-ass stare butted him away.

"The set is over," said Isis.

"Thank God. That bitch has more alcohol in her voice than melody." A couple of heads at a nearby table turned, but I didn't give a shit.

"Chico says that somebody else is singing in the second set. 'Hot' talent. So it does not matter."

She wasn't cringing as much at my vulgarity, and her eyes still looked all glowy, as strange as I felt, holding the thing inside me from taking me over and maybe, fuck it all, doing to Isis what Isis had done to Cleopachra. She leaned in and I smelled her vanilla and jasmine scent, pheromones for the men around, Chico and that black dude.

"Fina," she hissed, "I need your help. Something bad happened to me today."

I spotted Chico on the stage. He was wearing the same creamy white single-breasted suit as the other musicians, except that his had shiny big satin lapels.

I turned to Isis quickly. "Okay, okay."

Chico came over to us smiling, and squeezed my hand. "How are you feeling, Fina? You look better." He examined my French manicured acrylics and said "Now that's the Fina I know." Then, just as soon as he was with us, he turned and went back on the stage.

"Chico," I called softly, but he didn't hear me.

I turned to Isis.

"Fina, a ghost is haunting me. I need you to do a *despojo* for me."

"A ghost?"

The orchestra started testing the instruments, saxes and trumpets squawking a few notes, the pianist playing scales.

A number Chico called "Gone City" started up, involving part of the orchestra, trumpets, piano, bass, alto sax, congas, timbales, bongos and maracas.

Chico's trumpet conversed with the sax. The sax wanted to lay back down and relax—hey, the city was like a dream. The trumpet wanted to go, go, go; the city's rhythm was out of control.

The *nfuiri* seemed to groove to the pulsing of the music, and I started to let both rhythms move me.

Who knows the city better? "I do!" bragged the trumpet.

"I told you about that woman, Fina. Remember?"

I didn't have to remember. "She's dead? Aurora?"

Isis' eyes were dark. "Chico talks about her." It wasn't a question. "Can you help me?"

Rhythmic dots sprouted all over my body, a web of energy, a cage made of fluid bars that the *nfuiri* was at times caressing, at times shaking.

"Yes, yes, yes, yes," I said because the rhythm that was coming from the *nfuiri* needed an outlet.

"Tomorrow in the morning we'll do it, we'll deal with it and lay it to rest. We will lay it to rest." And the *nfuiri* drew back and the web got looser.

Isis nodded. "I need a *despojo* to clean her from me."

"Yes, tomorrow morning."

And then a familiar voice chimed in: "Chica, but doesn't a *despojo* take weeks to prepare? Don't be sloppy with your *fufús*. That could get you in trouble."

Out on the part of the stage closest to us came Alba dressed in one of those long glittering gowns that only Hollywood starlets and nightclub singers wear. Silver with lavender sequins. She was wearing a black fur hat that looked too big for her.

"You better pay Fina real good for that." The girl's little rosebud mouth laughed, but her eyes were dull and black, like rubber that you could fingertip, leaving a mark. Her hair was short and had been done in waves, so now she did look like a ghoulish version of Betty Boop.

"Where the hell have you been?" I asked her. She laughed. Then she twirled, and the gown revealed her back down to the cleft in her buttocks. Her Ivory soap skin was kind of mesmerizing, I had to admit.

Chico came up to her on the stage, and she reached up and flicked something off Chico's shiny lapel.

I turned to Isis. "Don't worry none about her. She's full of shit."

"Just like her mother," said Isis.

"Ahh," I cupped my chin in one hand. "So she is Aurora's daughter?"

Isis shrugged.

The new set started. Chico introduced the girl as "The talented and *young* Alba Sánchez." And, before he could go on to re-introduce the lead musicians and the orchestra, the girl took the microphone from him and squeaked, "And I want to say how happy I am to be playing with the fabulous trumpet player Chico de León." Alba tipped her fur hat. "Ohmigod, I am so happy!"

Then the girl, who was short even in her high heels, stood on her tippy toes, exaggeratedly pursed her lips and kissed Chico on the mouth. To his credit, he moved so that the kiss landed on his chin. The crowd applauded enthusiastically, but a few people made hooting noises.

"What I really want to know is if she's Chico's daughter?"

"What do you think, Fina?"

I ordered a Long Island Ice Tea. When it came, I sipped it slowly, then leaned over and tapped my fingers on the iron railing, trying to see if I could catch Chico's eye.

The girl sang a song with just the piano for background. Some of the musicians were following, reading the music from their music stands. When she was done with that song, she started a new one. This time she was singing to Chico's trumpet. It was "Love Migrates," and people started to cheer.

A few notes into it, Chico announced it as his composition.

"You are my destiny," sang the girl, her voice mellow, sad and jaunty too. "That's why you don't have to love me back."

The trumpet answered sadly, "Don't, don't, don't love me, tuturuturu, you don't have to love me back."

"The man you love doesn't have to love you back . . . " sang the girl.

"Don't, never, don't, never, don't, have to love her back," trilled the trumpet defiantly and happily.

And then the saxes came in. "This love ain't happening, and maybe it's better that way, this love wasn't meant to be, and that's a good thing, too. This love is moving away, moving, moving, away," lamented the alto.

The bass sax seemed to argue, "I won't let it go, no, no, no."

The alto pointed out, "It'll go no matter what you do."

And then in conversation, bass and alto, the alto first. "Let it go." The bass, "Oh, no." The alto, "It's going anyway." The bass, "Oh, no. Oh, oh."

The trumpet came in again loud and obnoxious, "Love migrates."

"Love is moving, moving away," observed the saxes.

"Migrate, migrate, love is migrating," blared the trumpet.

"This migrating was part of our destiny. Real love can't stay the same . . . " sang the girl regretfully.

Fuck, she was good. The depressing song made me grin like an idiot, and the *nfuiri* was soft in me, soft and floating, not driving outward or kernelling inward, almost happy.

"Love migrates, it's just not meant to stay the same," raged the trumpet.

"Love migrates, it just moves away, love migrates, it just can't stay the same . . . " The girl was dismissing the old love, even as she welcomed a new one.

And the trumpet: angry and yet matter of fact, answered that this was the way life was, "Don't get hung up on it. I'm leaving now, I'm moving away. Will I come back? Yes, maybe some day. But now? Love migrates." The trumpet notes fled, impetuous and vindicated. And the piano sadly affirmed with crystalline final notes that love was no longer here to stay.

The girl tipped her hat again, this way, and again that way. I suddenly realized her hat was a fedora.

"A super composition by Chico de León, the best music of the night, which he humbly waited for the second set to play."

Chico, his eyes shining, waved at me and Isis. The crowd went wild with applause.

Isis and I approached the stage. Isis kissed Chico on the mouth and congratulated him, and while they slobbered over each other, I ran backstage.

Next, I don't know what the fuck happened because the little bitch was nowhere to be seen, and the musicians backstage all refused to tell me where she'd gone, like I was a freaking stalker.

Okay, so maybe I got *some* stalker in me. After all, I found the hat in a hamper next to the mirrors. On the hat's inside brim were two small labels. One said, "Genuine mink," and the other, "Adolfa Alegría Hornedo." I didn't know Victor's ex-wife from Adam, but I'd take odds any day that name was Cuban, not Rican. And that the hat was Genio's fedora.

EIGHT
FLORIDA WATER

I pushed open the *botánica* door, glancing quickly at the tor- toises paddling helplessly in the glass aquarium.

Behind the counter, the walls were lined in shelves contain- ing all kinds of figures, from blue plaster virgins to wooden statues of slaves in chains, old Haitian farmers, porcelain Kwan Yins and Buddhas.

"Josefina, ju de person I want to see today!" said Perla, and her gold tooth glinted. Her million-year-old face was shrunken like a prune, and the odor of the dye she used to turn her white hair black crisped my nose hairs.

Anybody was always the person Perla wanted to see, as long as you bought something. "I need Florida water."

"Ju know, der is only one bottle left."

"One is all I need."

"I haf good customers today. Someone come and buy all de Florida Water. Emagine dat."

"Cleansings, curses, *despojos*—this neighborhood is hop- ping with *fufús*."

"Den dey come back and give back one, das de one for you."

"*¡Fantástico!*" I glanced at the shelves with rows of boxes with names like Yo Puedo y Tú No, Money, Juan Conquistador, Bed of Roses; the stands with necklaces in multi- colored beads representing saints, *orishas*, *nkisis*; the rows of rusted railroad nails on the floor next to the glass case, on top of which sat the cash register. Then I darted a glance at the backroom.

Before I even said anything, Perla said, "Next week. Today, nothing good in back. Emagine dat."

So here I was preparing the *fufú* of all *fufús*, the *fufú* that my rival really wanted, the *fufú* that she felt was going to free her of fear and that I knew was finally going to free me of her.

I was dead certain. I had always really wanted to believe in my spells, and now I had found this *nfuiri*. When I wasn't flying over the world, or spearing deep into the heart of time and memory to discover that there was after all a beyond, I suddenly missed the wooziness, the craziness of it, like being high from booze, sex, drugs. But purer. After all, for years I had thought that these out-of-body, out-of-mind phenomena, so to speak, were just part of my everyday need to get over.

I had thought I was faking it, but now I think that the line between pretending and believing isn't so clear. Belief was like a fancy dress I'd always stopped myself from trying on because I thought it would feel tight and wrong. I was learning that not only was this elegance within reach, but that the sense of freedom I felt was, for the first time, internal.

Maybe that's why when Isis showed up later at my place with the boxes of candles—hundreds of candles of all kinds, votives, tapers, glass encased—I was startled to hear myself say, "I made a *baño* to refresh you." I pointed to the bathroom.

"*Ay*, Fina, you are a marvel." Isis blew a kiss that was like her salute to the public as Miss Universe, and then she closed the bathroom door behind her.

I went into my bedroom, gargled with the over-proof rum straight from the bottle and spat out into the cauldron. Then I lit a cigar and smoked out in long curling puffs over the cauldron. I tapped my left foot three times: "*Nganga nfuiri bakiakuantala*, make Isis Sandín leave. Quickly. And purify her, for this she really needs." I nodded and started a chant under my breath: "*Nsambia* says, but *Palo* does. *Mayombe dice y Palo hace. Para bien y para mal . . .*"

In the bathroom, Isis' jeans, top and lacy underthings were piled on the floor next to the tub. On top I noticed one of those little folder things that they give you at hotels for your card key.

Isis rose up a bit, still sitting in the tub, and took the cup of tea from my hands. She sipped and closed her eyes. "All my evils are washing away from me."

I picked up the little folder and opened it, making sure she didn't see me. "1511" was written at the top. I flicked the little folder shut and I perched my large ass as comfortably as I could on the toilet lid.

Isis put her tea cup down on the cracked floor tiles and sank back in the tub.

"The bath will make me stronger . . . more attractive. But who knows?" A dreamy look came into her eyes. "When I was young and lonely, so lonely shut up in that house in Vega Baja, I took a bath like this one. I attracted a boy right away."

She'd been a girl who felt she was suffocating in an old house all shuttered from the sun. She crushed Madonna lilies picked at dew time and put them in her panties to attract love.

"He showed up the day after I took the bath, the son of one of my father's friends. After I was allowed to go out with him, I was not so lonely."

She cradled her head in one elbow, pulling her long black hair out of the tub with her other hand. Tendrils of uncaught hair curled onto her neck.

I half-closed my eyes. Isis went on with her shadowy story.

Isis strolled on the Vega Baja beach one night with the boy. He gave her a sloppy smoocheroo. Then he started feeling her up with big starfish hands. Finally, he pulled her down.

When she saw his thing gray and wet like a mollusk inching out of the sand, Isis laughed.

Isis pulled her body out of the water with a splash. She stood, pointing at something behind my head.

"What? What?" I looked behind me. The narrow window in the bathroom wall was shut tight because of the cold. There was nothing there.

I turned back to Isis and couldn't help staring at her shaved pubis. Not because I'm a lezzie, mind you. I think most people have a little homo and just go for the straight if it's stronger. In me the straight is stronger. But it was almost like Isis' body was asking me to look and look. Her vulva bulged like a cat's eye. I wondered if Chico liked for her to shave there. Sort of like Gus, who had always asked me to get a Brazilian, but I never would. Bury your face in my forest, into my coral reef, I'd command. But his dips and dives were pretty damn grudging.

"I saw it . . . again," spluttered Isis.

"Shadow. Angles in the wall."

"No, it was a face."

I handed her a towel.

"I have been having this image in my head. A face I don't know. The sockets are empty in the face. But the empty sockets stare at me."

"Like a skull." I pointed out. Well, that was the skull and bones in any cauldron. So it was the *nfuiri* she was seeing?

But what did she mean "again"?

"Isis, did that boy rape you?"

"He left me on the beach. I walked home in the night. It took me all night. When I got back, my father knocked me against the shelves." Isis imitated the swing of her father's arm, her breasts quivering and the naked skin of her belly stung in tiny bumps.

"One of Mami's Lladró figures went crashing to the floor." Her eyes narrowed. "I always hated those stupid figurines. I wanted to throw another one at the wall. I wish I had done it."

Anybody who wanted to show they had a little extra money on the island liked to display those pastel blue and white Lladró statuettes.

"I'm surprised you don't like Lladró."

"Lladró figures look all the same." Isis stared at me, her eyes big and golden. "You know, Fina, we are alike. We appear like the others that we grew up with. But we are not like them. Maybe we can be friends?"

"Ain't we friends?" I muttered and looked away because I could tell that I had turned red.

And then I got mad at myself, stuttering and blushing like a kid, something that was happening a lot these days.

She didn't push it. Anyway, so we both hated Lladrós, so what? We both liked Chico, too. Liking the same thing can lead to love. Or hate. Or maybe love *seasoned with a pinch of hate. Amor con odio* like they said in Puerto Rico.

She went on with the story. "Mami picked up every last little slice of porcelain. She cut herself and started calling me a *puta*."

I shook my head. "Did you tell them . . . ?"

"Tell them what? That their dear friend's son showed me his curly worm? The boy would not talk to me, he was humiliated. That is why he left me on the beach."

She shuddered, and her breasts jiggled. "I walked all night, but the walk back wasn't so bad. I stayed in the shadows of the palm trees, trying not to be noticed by the passing cars of the *cocolos—real* men." She looked me in the eyes.

I gave her a towel. She stood up. Crouching slightly, she patted herself casually between the legs.

"Fina, that boy couldn't have raped me even if he had tried."

By the time she came out of the bathroom, I'd lit all fifty or so of the glass-encased candles and set them out on the dinette and end tables, on my speakers and the floor. If it hadn't been in daylight, the place would have looked like a scene in one of them horror movies where the crazy-devil-possessed-psycho-stalker lights up hundreds of candles before confronting the victim.

Now just because I'm a witch, and maybe a voyeur, doesn't mean that I'm psycho or that I'm interested in commerce with Satan, or any of that horror movie crap. The devil has an equivalent in *Palo*—Lukankanse—but I ain't interested in that *nkisi*, nor is Tata Victor, and we don't mix with the people who are.

In hindsight, I think I could have given a little more thought to the symbol and metaphor stuff, what the *nfuiri* stood for, as smart girl Shellman might have said. But I hold that at that moment I just wanted to step in and do my neat flying out of my big fat body and seeing other people's lives. My little secret. My dream world. And I needed to find out more about my father. And, yeah, I wanted to run Isis out of town.

Homegirl came out of the bathroom in the white skirt and T-shirt I'd asked her to wear. She had also turbaned a white towel around her hair. She sat on the little stool in the corner of the dining area where I'd tacked white sheets to the wall.

I had been muttering for a long time to the bones in the cauldron, asking them to help me see what would make Isis leave. So, even as she accommodated herself on the stool, I was stepping in.

It was fast, maybe the *nfuiri* couldn't wait no more. The image came pretty clear. Isis. She was naked, the same body I'd just seen in the tub, maybe a waspier waist, naked. She was holding a woman in her arms. A *mulata* with the heart-shaped face I'd seen in the photo in Chico's night table. And the famously gold kinked hair.

A man was fucking the *mulata*. I could only see him from the back, a man with a big floppy ass. White as larva. Yucko. But he looked familiar. Maybe because those short fat male builds are real common on the island. They usually go with black mustachios and promises such as "Don't worry. We'll fix things. Nobody will know."

Isis was holding Aurora so that the fat man could fuck her. But she was kissing her, too. And Aurora arched her back. Pleasure, pleasure from both sides—and Isis held her tight.

Suddenly, all I saw was fire, fire eating up the underbush, flames jumping. And through the long serpent tongue licks of flame, hands, blackened charred hands.

I was staring at Isis now. She was grabbing at her neck and yelling, "I feel hot, like in hell!"

I put out a hand, I don't know why, actually.

She pushed me off.

Isis opened her knees wide and leaned her torso over one knee. Her eyes were almost black now.

"Rita hungry now. Rita killed, and angry."

I looked at Isis, but I knew it wasn't Isis. Shit. Aurora?

"Who is Rita?"

"Here," said Isis. Isis' hands touched her throat. "And here." Her hands pointed to her heart. "And here." The hands clasped Isis' face and snaked like a belly dancer's through her hair up to the top of her head. Then she stayed with her arms like that, hugging her head and smiling a little.

"You are Rita, but you are in Isis now?"

The *nfuiri* laughed at my stupid fucking question.

Isis, or rather her body, got up from the stool, dropping her arms. Her walk, almost a limp that made her ass wiggle a bit, conjured up someone who was used to wearing tight skirts, someone raunchier than Isis and completely confident in the allure of her raunchiness. Someone who preferred to walk barefoot on a beach, feeling the sand massage her toes, someone who loved to dance, who could fuck all night every night, who now wanted to eat and drink her fill.

"Rita hungry now. Bring me eggs."

"Your name is Rita?"

"Bring me eggs now, I say."

"Eggs? Wait. I need to cook them."

"Now! Rita hungry now!"

"Well, you know, uncooked eggs ain't healthy."

But I went to the refrigerator and took out a pink foam carton of eggs.

In the dining space, Rita was touching her breasts. With a grin of surprise on her face, she pinched one of her nipples through the white T-shirt Isis had put on and laughed when it hardened into a pointy cone. She was like a child enchanted by a toy, and the toy was Isis' body. Her hands slid to her stomach, and over the white cloth she squeezed a handful of belly with her fingers as if it were dough.

"Soft," she smiled. "Fat!"

"Well, not too bad." I automatically sucked in my own stomach.

"Good fat." Rita leered at me through the mask of Isis' face.

Then the hands went to Isis' body's hips and thighs. The *nfuiri* started to hum low. "*A la nanita nana nanita eha . . .* " An old lullaby in Spanish. "*Nanita eha . . . nanita eha . . .* "

Not a bad voice, but she stopped before I could gain a full appreciation.

Her nostrils flared. "The horse is the most beautiful."

"Yes," I said. "She is beautiful."

"I love the horse."

"That's nice."

I picked an egg from the carton. The insides shifted, and I handed it to her.

Isis, or Rita, brought the egg to her mouth, cracked it with one hand and licked the slimy insides from it. Then she snatched the pink carton, took another egg and cracked it. She noisily sucked out the insides, enjoying this one more greedily than the first, slurping up even some of the shell fragments. She ate all eight eggs that were left in the carton, cracking them with one hand, sucking up the goo and then flicking most of the eggshell from her mouth like a snake.

I was trying to phrase my "Who the hell are you really?" in a way an *nfuiri* might feel like answering, when she asked me for rum.

I did think about it twice, but then she growled, "Rum, *carajo!*" So I brought her Bacardi Gold, the best rum I had, but not the strongest.

Isis, or Rita, didn't seem to mind that it wasn't 151-proof. She chugged it down without blinking.

"Now is now. Now is for Rita. Fina bring Florida water."

"You know my name?"

"Rita know Fina. Rita chose Fina."

"Why? And for what"

"To clean the horse," she said. "To clean the house! All the house!"

"What?"

"Drink Florida water!"

"Yes, Rita, yes." I rushed to bring out the Florida water bottle that I had been saving for the end of the ritual.

Rita snatched the bottle of Florida water out of my hands. Then she put the neck inside her mouth and chugged. She spat it out, almost gagging on it. "Rita burn water out," she said.

"I know." I wanted to be gentle, but I needed to be firm too. An *nfuiri* using someone else's body for speaking purposes was like a kindergartner. "Are you Aurora?"

Rita took the bottle of Florida water and poured half of it over Isis' head, and then the rest of it over her arms and breasts, her hips and thighs. "Rita."

Rita swung one hip and then the other, making Isis' body churn her belly seductively. "I am Rita." Then she threw out her arms, as if grasping an invisible dancing partner, and moved Isis' head of mussed hair from side to side. Throughout her dancing to invisible music, Rita still touched Isis' body everywhere with her fingers and palms. Sometimes she smacked it hard with her open hand.

Then she started pinching herself harder.

Something occurred to me. "Aurorita? Who called you that?"

The invisible music changed, and Isis' body now danced a circling rhythm faster and faster until she bumped into the candles on the floor.

"Now I am Rita!" When Isis' skirt caught fire, Rita didn't stop.

Flames tore at the garment, and I screamed and rushed towards Isis. The white skirt suddenly grew a series of sizzling flounces.

I grabbed at Isis' arm, gagging on the sudden smell of roast beef. Isis turned quick, and her skirt started to burn my jeans.

"Throw yourself on the floor!" I said, doing so myself, rolling around until I'd tamped the flames from my jeans.

I don't know if Isis could hear me at that point. Her clothes started to shrink and burn off her body, revealing the boiled skin below, but still her body moved jerkily, and her eyes watered over their red rims.

I went to the kitchen, pulled open the cabinet under the kitchen sink, fumbled through pots and pans. I breathed in, and felt a stinging in my lungs.

Smoke. I filled a big pot with water from the tap and ran towards Isis. Her body whirled in imperfect circles and I smelled the sickening odor of burnt hair before I saw locks of her hair sparked like coals. I threw water at her hair, but I was so close to her that the steam burned my hand, and I dropped the pot. The flames growled all over Isis.

"Please, stop it. Stop it, Rita. You're fanning the flames. Stop moving!"

Isis' body writhed and burned, bumping against cabinets and knocking down framed pictures, DVDs, statuettes and bowls. She hit her head against walls and door jambs. Like a tarred mechanical doll gone haywire, like the blackened bird devoured by ants, she was knocking about faster and faster the closer she looked to being dead.

I ran to the bedroom, pulled off a sheet from the bed and stumbled back into the dining area.

That stench of burning meat overcame me, and I choked on the smoke. My legs buckled and I went down. Then I was on the ground, on top of the sheet, grasping my throat. I looked up. The stumbling Isis sent most of the glass candle jars on one shelf crashing to the floor. She crunched glass under her shoe.

A wound opened on Isis' face and I saw pink spongy tissue. But Isis seemed to grin wider and spin faster. Why didn't Rita react to the wound? Or to the way the fire consumed Isis' flesh?

She was an *nfuiri*. Couldn't she feel all of the things a body felt? She liked the eggs and rum, and the touching of Isis' body. Why could she feel the pleasure and not the pain?

I got up, stumbled, found the sheet I had dropped at the threshold to the bedroom and dragged it with me. I was struggling to reach the phone, but a thick haze filled the room, and now it wasn't just that it was hard to breathe, it was hard to move, too. I heard knocking and muffled shouting in the hall, but couldn't find the door in the smoke.

Finally, I grasped the phone. But when I heard the 911 operator, I could barely get out, "She . . . she's going . . . "

"Ma'am, ma'am, could you repeat that? Ma'am, give me your address."

"Help me!" My lungs gave out, and I doubled over. The receiver slipped out of my hand. I kept my head up looking at Isis.

She was lying face-up on the knocked over candles on the kitchen table. Some of the candles had gone out, but there was an amber flow of light under her body.

Everywhere in the apartment, and inside me, the smell bloomed, a smell of cooked and thickly oozing flesh. My lungs felt like they were burning and bleeding all at once.

Isis' blackened vibrating features seemed twisted into a grin.

Then I realized that Rita could feel the pain of Isis' body. Wasn't that the point?

The skin over one of Isis' eyes had oozed shut, but the other was fused open, staring at me, until I went blind.

NINE

THE ROOM

There was knocking at the door, then shouting. The door rattled in its frame. Then: tapa, tapa, tapa. The zinc roof in the storm? Hec, hec, hec. With each breath I felt my lungs tear, and there was a throbbing in my fingers, almost like the skin had burned off the bones.

A crashing sound, then muscle-bound giants in uniform pounded on the floorboards. Firemen and policemen loomed blurrily.

"Two bodies! One's alive. The other . . . Jesus!"

"Got this one." Oxygen tank, stretcher. Commotion and whispering.

I tried to move. One of the giants squatted down, and told me not to. Sunburn in winter: skier, paramedic.

A woman with glasses, another paramedic with an oxygen tank, scissors and a large bottle of water, knelt down. "I'm going to cut the shirt pieces off. Is there anybody else here beside the two of you?"

Hec, hec, hec.

"No."

The woman with the glasses peeled off the charred cotton on my arms. "We're pouring water on your body so the burns won't cook any further." Water like a blessing on my hands, a mask on my nose. Breathe, breathe.

"What happened?"

A familiar voice, a neighbor? More people trying to come in.

"Is she all right?" Old Virgil from upstairs.

"Stand away from the door, sir." Policeman.

"What is your name, ma'am?" Mask pulled off to let me speak.

Loud male voice. "Neighbor says her name is Josephine."

"Josephine, what happened?" The woman's glasses like small moons, cool hands.

"I didn't tell her."

"You didn't tell her what? Josephine?"

"That we could try . . . " I gasped for air.

"Maybe you didn't have to tell her," said the paramedic with cool and gentle hands.

Many hands under me now, the crowd of capable giants heaved me onto the stretcher. My bones felt like a bag of broken glass.

Slow, deep, breathe in. "Cauldron."

"Calm down, ma'am." The paramedic put her cool hand on my boiling forehead. "What? What is it?" Slipping the mask to the side again.

I lifted my head. "Cauldron . . . bedroom . . . check."

"What does she want?"

"Please . . . bedroom." I made an effort and pushed off the stretcher, and my body, dead weight that I couldn't steer any more, fell crashing at the threshold of the door.

Drumbeats of pain in my head and hands. "Please."

"Jesus Christ." The skier paramedic lifted me now, a fireman helped.

"See if there's a fucking witch's cauldron in her bedroom!"

The woman medic with the glasses ran.

The skier and the firemen hefted me back onto the stretcher, wheeled me out to the ambulance and it was that gray time right before dusk. I saw the moon, all nibbled, with a shadow for an iris.

The medic now looked at me through the double moon of her glasses. "Relax, we found it, now just relax. It's fine, it's in the bedroom, a cauldron with your plants inside. They're alive, don't worry."

Whenever I opened my eyes, they would ask about the pain. They were giving me morphine for the pain. Honey-voiced Filipino nurses spoke to me in Spanish: *¿Cómo estás?; ¿Tienes dolor?*

Chico came twice, his face drawn, eyes bloodshot. The last time he left white roses that quickly unfurled petals, and were dead the next day.

Victor brought a giant arrangement of star-gazer lilies and birds of paradise.

I tried to tell him about Rita.

He grabbed my hand, stared into my eyes: "Forget about it for now. Just rest. We'll talk later."

A nurse's aide read me a magazine article: "What Men Find Irresistible (It's Not What You Think!)," and I put up a hand.

Alba didn't come, but why would she? She'd been my roommate for just a few weeks.

A narrow window, lowered blinds; night gray, day gray, perpetual twilight. Eyes closed, half-lidded, the chair, the night lamp, the moving nurse almost as distant as the world outside the window.

A singing group appeared on Christmas Eve afternoon, and I fell asleep almost as soon as they started "Silent Night."

A man with a pale face and gray eyes asked me what happened. The detective on the case. I wasn't a suspect yet, the burns on my hands showed that I tried to help.

"Tell me about the gasoline."

I said, groggily, "Gasoline?"

"Tell me what happened."

I couldn't talk about Rita; they wouldn't know what to say, much less do, about Rita. Maybe they'd put me in the booby hatch after I recovered from the burns. I wanted to fall back, away from the questions. I wanted coolness for the burning: trees, trees whispering around me.

I was in the park, walking quickly. I looked at the iron Victorian lamps lining the path. Their lady bodies and luminous shades were the only planets visible in this night. I stopped. I didn't know what the time was, and this wasn't any part of the park that I recognized. I hurried along. I knew I had to get somewhere, but where?

There was a green light ahead. Green, like lichen on a rock. I stumbled on a tree root. This was not a well-kept park path. It was overgrown with frost-choked creepers and fallen branches, and the trees on each side of the path leaned over almost meeting. Still, I followed, trying not to look at the trees now, half alive with malice, whispering: "You killed her, couldn't tell her, didn't want to, Papi gone or dead in some apartment somewhere, and Genio died too. . . . "

I reached what looked like the top of a hill, and the green light wavered and then vanished. I could see in the darkness now: different trees with silvery trunks, as wide as the stone and mortar gatehouse, which they surrounded. The roots sprung out like tentacles grasping the bottom edges of the building, snaking up the stone walls.

The narrow door said "1511." I pushed it open.

The morning of the day they released me, the cop came back and sat next to my bed.

"There were traces of gasoline in the Florida water bottle. Or what was left of it."

He had scrubbed pink skin and curly, light brown hair. Looked of German descent—had an Italian last name.

"Did you know her boyfriend bought up all the Florida water in that botánica you all go to?"

"What? Chico?"

The cop's sandy eyebrows went up with his nod.

"What did he say?"

"We can't find him right now, Miz Mata."

"But he was just here visiting . . . just last week."

"I know," he stopped and smiled. For a cop, he was pretty gentle. He was probably putting on a "good cop" routine. "I think there's something you're not telling us."

My throat felt constricted. I looked away, then back at him wondering if I should talk about my crush.

"What made Isis throw herself on the candles? Was she suicidal? Was she upset about something?"

"She was seeing things."

"What kinds of things?"

"A ghost."

"A ghost?" His eyelids fluttered, and then his eyes became very expressive—like he wanted to laugh—but he tried to keep a straight face. "Well, some Hispanics swear by these cleansing rituals."

I closed my eyes. My hand throbbed. I wanted more morphine in the drip.

Thick tree roots veined and wound along the floor of the room. A tree canopy and the starless night sky shone through the roofless top.

I stepped forward but the dirt floor gave way and I fell into a hole, on clay that smelled of arum lilies and shit. And moldy bones.

I turned. Bones still wearing rags of a white dress, gold kinked hair tufting out of one of the empty holes that had been her eyes.

The skull opened its bony jaw to speak: "Take me to the water."

The January world outside the hospital made me feel as if I'd been an inmate for six months, not a few weeks. There had been no snow. Now the air was too warm for it. The glaring sunlight shrank the brick façades of Manhattan valley.

Somebody had forgotten to take down the Christmas lights framing the building's door.

In spite of the open window, the smell of melted plastic and deep smoke hit me as soon as I opened the door. I felt a little wave of nausea thicken and close off my throat, so I went to the bathroom to wash my face.

Back in the living room, I saw the superintendent's men had put down a new wood floor, painted my apartment a grayish white and swept away the glass from *bóveda* cups and candleholders and all the other sooty shit. The furniture was still there: the cheap dining table with crumpled legs, the TV with its exploded screen like a retro seventies sculpture, the cloth sofa burned in a spitting kapok pattern.

That German-looking cop who'd come to the hospital told me that the police had snatched all medications, liquids and perfumes, because they wanted to see if there was gasoline in any other containers. They'd also taken clothes, kitchenware and plates, for DNA testing.

I was now in the clear because of the burns on my hands and face, which showed I tried to help Isis. And Perla said that Chico had bought all the Florida water bottles and then brought one back.

In the bedroom, the sides of the cauldron were burned black and peeling. There was just a handful of dirt near the bedroom's baseboard. Incredibly, the stripling *palos* were still green.

I didn't have time to feed her the blood of a chicken, and she was so dry she'd need blood soon. But I thought of the little hotel card on the pile of her clothes, and I knew where I had to go.

It was getting gusty when I got to the Carlyle. Pearl pink clouds were banking up in the winter sky.

The lobby of the hotel was all black marble, coral leather and mirrors, mirrors everywhere. I looked into a gigantic mirror and panicked when I couldn't find myself.

A guy all dressed in bright blue and a bowler hat with white gloves tapped me on the shoulder. "Can I help you?"

"Shee-it, the fuckers at the studio cancelled on me, and now I'm just waiting for a callback, dude." My extensions clicked and clacked like castanets.

He nodded, and walked off.

I walked up to room 1511 just as Alba was opening the door for Chico.

She wore a black wool skirt with horizontal pockets and a white silk top and was barefoot, one foot hitched up on the opposite knee. She folded her arms and smirked when she saw me. Chico turned and for a moment didn't seem to recognize me.

How could such a puzzled face hide such a rat?

I looked from him to Alba, and then I slapped him.

He blinked, like he didn't really feel or care about the slap, and I barreled past him. When I caught a look at him again, it was like his face started to melt this way and that, and his expression made Alba burst into peals of laughter.

The room was no room in the normal sense. To me it was more like palatial holdings—parquet floors, a kind of tea reception area, a huge chandelier like a crystal ship floating over white leather sofas and armchairs. The grand piano seemed like it was the size of two refrigerators. To my left were three closed wooden doors. What I liked the most was what I saw through the glass French doors: a balcony as big as my bedroom overlooking the greenery on the east side of Central Park.

"This is where Isis was staying?" I turned to Alba. "Why are *you* here?

Chico's face was pale, his voice icy: "You fucked-up runt. You asked me to get those bottles. You said it was for a cleansing. You fucking lied to me."

He made a sudden dash at her, slapping widely with his hands, and she scooted behind a white whale of a couch.

He paced to the right near one end of the couch. Alba moved to the back left of the couch, and then Chico backpedaled to the left front. "Did you put gasoline in the bottle you asked me to take back? Because if you did . . . "

"It's true what they say. Musicians are pretty fucking stupid." Alba's eyes were hooded, but a big shit eating grin took over her face. And she stuck her tongue at him as she started to move to the back right corner of the couch.

Chico scrambled over the couch, caught Alba by the waist and grabbed at her shirt. She tried to bite him, but he jerked away, still grabbing at her shirt, which tore. She screamed with glee like a kid on a playground and ran around the right corner of the couch, but then she knocked her shin into a glass coffee table and cursed a string of shit even I had never heard. She ran to one of the bedroom doors. But Chico who had headed towards the bedrooms from the closer left-hand side of the couch got there first and grabbed her by the throat. He pressed both hands around her neck and started strangling her.

Alba's face went red and she opened her mouth and tried to take in air. Chico snarled at that, looking like he himself was being choked.

A bedroom door opened.

A short, fat man stood there with a gun, which he pointed at Chico. "Get your hands off of her, *mijo.*"

Chico pulled his hands off of Alba's throat and turned to face the fat man. "Of course, I should have known. You." He spat on the parquet floor, then wiped his mouth.

Alba pressed a hand to each side of her bruised neck and started a kind of mirthless giggling.

The fat guy was wearing a fucking smoking jacket! Movie velvet. Under that: flannel pants, and a formal white shirt. His old face and hands were pasty white. Hairy hands, but the nails looked perfectly groomed. I could smell the expensive perfume on him: moss, leather, the kind of whispery flowers that grow near rivers.

He beamed at me, happy as Santa. "Hello, Miss Mata."

I cocked my head. "I've seen you somewhere."

The man came a little closer and put out one of those pale hands covered in long black hair. But he kept his gun trained on Chico.

I hesitated. I would have had to move closer to take his hand, and I didn't want to move away from Chico, who stood stock still. Then Chico's features contorted, and his eyes got small and beady.

"I should have fucking known." Chico's voice was thick. "Don't touch him, Fina. The guy is poison. His family owns half of Puerto Rico, and the people, too."

I realized now that the fat man had to be Senator Ferrera. But I didn't really remember him from the island newspapers, which I hadn't read since I was a girl. Where had I seen that face?

Chico glanced quickly at both ends of the narrow space in which he stood, and then he stepped towards Ferrera. "Isis was going to leave you, finally, after all these years. You couldn't take it, could you?"

"Hold it right there, *mijo*. Why must we get so upset? That's not necessary. Let us relax, sit down and converse. Why get so flustered?" If anything, the guy's smile got bigger, showing the whitest pearlies in the world, as if for him this was an everyday type of social situation.

And then I realized he was the ugly man I'd seen with Alba on the night of Isis' birthday party.

"Converse with you? You ain't about conversing, Ferrera. You're about lying and stealing. And killing, too, when you have to. You know what? I don't give a shit if you shoot me." Chico tried to step closer to Ferrera but Ferrera moved past the threshold of the bedroom door. "'Cause your bullets can't hurt me anymore."

"Well, then, I may just end up shooting her," said Ferrera almost casually. He now trained the gun on me. "It really makes no difference. You are all more or less the same to me." And his big old charming smile showed what seemed like rows and rows of his perfectly white teeth.

Chico stopped, looked at me and then at Ferrera. The sound that came from his mouth was a short bark. "I hate you, Ferrera. I hate your family. I hate the millions that you steal from the colony. I hate how you control half the island like a plantation. I hate your maggot-white skin. I hate your TV gossip and music shows that distract islanders from the fact that the Ferreras make up what people think. I hate the way you sweet-talk the people you fuck over. I hate your fat little body. I hate your make-believe legacy of newspapers and shopping malls. I hate your hairy hands. I hate . . . "

"*Mijo*, please! Let's come to an agreement, if only for the sake of your friend here." Ferrera was smiling so hard that his cheeks were round and bunched and rosy. But the gun was trained on me.

He walked a few paces over to me and squeezed my hand real tight with the hand that wasn't holding the gun. The hairy, wet, warmth of his hand made me realize how cold mine were, even though my face was hot. I wasn't afraid, though. It didn't seem to me Ferrera really wanted to shoot me. He just didn't want to have to shoot Chico.

I tried to quickly tighten my grip on his hand, wondering if I could throw the guy to the ground, but he seemed to know what I was thinking, let go of my hand and moved back quick, aiming the gun at my breasts and winking at me, enchanted by his notion that life was just one big joke played by God and the Ferrera family.

Chico breathed in and out hard. "Fina, I should have known. Ferrera had to be behind it. Alba was a patsy. He had her get in good with me, and get me to buy those bottles. He put the gasoline in that bottle!"

"No, he didn't." Alba put her hands on her hips, her chin lifted high, one eyebrow crooked quizzically, as if she had been picking flower arrangements for a celebration and had now realized she had selected the wrong store. "I wanted to get old Isis. She killed my mother. It's real sad you couldn't figure that shit out. Stu-pid! No wonder Mami dumped your ass."

Now there was only a faint smile pinned to her face, and her eyes glittered like onyx.

"Isis kill Aurora? She would never do something like that! And don't keep lying and saying Aurora was your mother." Chico bared his teeth.

Alba cocked her head like a bird. "But she was my mother. Old stingy Titi Jahaira wouldn't have raised me if I wasn't her niece." She sidled up to Ferrera, and grabbed his hairy hand, passing her fingers lightly over the muzzle of the gun. "And he's my papi."

Ferrera kept the gun pointed at me, glancing out of the corner of his eye at her and smiling slightly, his chest all puffed up with pride.

It was true that they were both the same larva-white color, and both had straight black hair, although Ferrera's looked suspiciously thick and wavy on the top of his head, like a mad Bosley. They both had the same dead, but driven, shark's eyes.

I looked at Chico, and could tell he was noticing the similarity, too. He closed his eyes, and opened his mouth to say something, but he couldn't.

"Isis and I agreed that she would go back to you. We also agreed that I could finally claim my child, after so many years. I'm proud of my only child," said Ferrera, caressing Alba's hair. "*La sangre llama.*"

A sudden gust of wind blew open the French doors. I felt dizzy and touched my head.

Chico looked at Alba, and laughed, joylessly, with his mouth open. Finally, he said slowly, "You're Ferrera's daughter? Looking at you both in the same room, I can see that now. You both got those ancient shark's eyes. But I don't understand. Aurora. My Aurora? How? How could that be?"

My chest started to get real hot, and I couldn't even feel my hands and arms.

"Blood will tell. Like at the place where the sea . . . " I mumbled. And then I fell.

I hadn't stepped in that I could recall, but I was flying past canopies of trees, a park, an unfamiliar park. There weren't any benches or lamps. And then I saw the ancient gray walls of a monastery, but as much as I wanted to linger, I couldn't. I had to keep on going until narrow brick buildings came into view, all built real close together. And then I saw a banner, or something like a banner, with a big yellow dragon on it.

I tried skimming over the ugly buildings, but instead I swooped low and examined the wooden bowls and trays and chopsticks in the store window. This had something to do with my father. And so did the dragon banner. But now I had to keep on going. The place where the river ran into the sea was much further away, much deeper back in time.

Then someone was patting my cheek, "Miss Fina, wake up, drink some brandy."

But I kept my eyes closed. I didn't want to wake up. Even though I was only poised on the edge of it, I wanted to go into that other world, and especially to that place, that place near the sea.

Now someone was putting a cool compress with a sea breezy smell on my forehead.

A sea breeze, yes. And now the place, the place where the river met the sea: a baby, ridiculously potbellied and double-chinned, played on the sand, and a woman with dark hair, burnt gold on the edges, watched her. The baby's black hair had been prettied up in pink and yellow ribbons, but somehow the ribbons made the kid look even uglier.

The baby played with little sticks and shells in the sand. Then the sand shifted under her, and she slid away. But the further she floated out to sea, the more the baby laughed, riding her sand horsey, giggling and waving, not afraid at all that she would drown.

Aurora ran in her white dress towards the baby and scooped her up with such force she almost fell herself.

"Where is the river?" I cried out. "The place where . . . "

Water gushed over me.

Alba was drying my neck, giggling a little, and they were all staring down at me.

I started touching my breasts frantically.

"What the fuck!" I hollered. "Who took off my bra?"

"You were asking for a river, girl," said Alba, still grinning and sitting at the foot of the bed with one of her melted black wax looks. "So I gave you one." Then she grabbed my hand. "No, seriously. For a second, we thought you were having a heart attack."

Chico was in a chair next to the door, his hands tied behind him. "Get her some water," he shouted.

"*Mijo*, keep your voice down," said Ferrera, beaming in his jolly way.

I sat up. I was in the most beautiful bedroom I'd ever seen, lying on a four poster mahogany bed done up in red covers and shit. There was a little writer's desk and chair on the opposite side of the room. Two sets of French doors led to a balcony that looked as ample as the one I'd seen when I walked into the suite.

A painting of a funeral procession marching through a desert somewhere hung over the desk. The painting was filled with golden colors, except for the coffin, which was covered in vibrant red cloth. On another wall there was a painting of a Saint Sebastian figure nailed to a door and wearing a loincloth in the same bright red color as the cloth covering the coffin in the first painting.

Ferrera was watching me intently. "Yes, they are by the same artist: Aldo Pagliacci, one of my favorites."

I was too woozy to try to get up and chest barrel Ferrera. Even if I'd been feeling up to it, he had the gun. So I let the part of myself that really did find something about the old goat charming take over. "I like the desert one."

"Ethiopia. You have good taste, Miss Mata," he said, all puffed up with pleasure, as if nothing else was going down at the moment.

"They're sad and beautiful."

And the balcony was even more beautiful. I could see it fully now, in the sunlight angling through the snow, just starting to flutter down. Trees, their naked branches glistening black through the snow, leaned over the balcony.

"This is Alba's room for now. Once she moves in with me on the island, she's getting an even bigger room." He reached a hand out to Alba, who got up off the bed and curled into Ferrera's arms. He gave her a good tight hug. I saw a look on her that I'd never seen before. Her eyes brightened.

"I'm going to go to this neat English-language school on the island," said Alba dreamily. "It's near the beach."

"I saw you in a dream I had. You were on a beach in Puerto Rico. With your mother."

She lifted her head from her father's chest. "Really?"

Out of the corner of my eye, I saw that Chico's brows were all in one strange hairy line, and his mouth was open.

Ferrera shot a look at him, his hand still holding the gun, and then looked at me. I shrugged.

I looked up at Chico again and saw that his mouth was twisted. And then I realized that he had just yelled.

He cried out again: "Really! Oh, really!" He was furious. "Are you out of your fucking mind flirting with this monster? Do you know that he owns half of Puerto Rico, that he wants to own the other half and that whoever gets in his way, he ruins? He tried to get his thugs to kill me years ago, made it so I could never go back. He had this bitch kid of his kill Isis, and then tried to make it seem like I did it."

"We don't know . . . " I tried to get up off the bed, but I felt a weird pressure on my neck, and blinked.

Ferrera shook his head at Chico, waving the gun a little.

"*Mijo,* don't you realize she's about to faint again? Your friend is not well. Why don't we let her recover, before we start dredging up ancient history?" He shook his head and looked at me again, smiling. "And, by the way, Miss Mata, Chico exaggerates. Yes, I am a wealthy man. Yes, I have business ventures. Yes, I wasn't pleased when Chico seduced my poor wife. But did I try to kill the man? Not likely. I don't kill. I can buy what I want. Killing is for the crowd. "

I really was dizzy, and having a hard time now following their back and forth.

In a kind of far-off shout, Chico accused Ferrera of not loving Isis, of marrying her only because she had been Miss Universe and Ferrera needed something pretty to hang on his arm since he himself was so fucking ugly. Then Ferrera, with nary a twitch of the lips or a blink of an eye, said very politely that Chico was a man with no family and no connections, who thought that a fling with a society woman could take him out of his clay barrio. Then Chico started yelling something about how Ferrera had gone looking for Aurora. Was that what had happened? Was that part of his revenge on Chico? Had he raped Aurora? Was that his revenge?

There was a black, melty look in Ferrera's eyes. I looked at Alba, then looked at Ferrera. "She's obviously your daughter," I whispered.

He looked at me again without really seeing me. "Yes, yes, she is," he murmured.

"Blood will tell." I mumbled. My mouth was dry and salty.

"We really don't want Miss Fina to faint away again, do we?" said Ferrera with that warmth of his that showed that he really was interested, as interested as anybody so fucking highborn could be. "Going into some other world."

A dizziness like fluttering fingers on my neck. I blinked. "Yeah," I started to agree. And then, again, that pressure at the base of my neck. I wanted that other world.

And then it occurred to me that if there was one thing a man like Ferrera couldn't control it was my dream world, my visions. "Like near the river."

"River?" said Ferrera.

My heart felt suddenly like a bird flying up against the bars of its cage. "It happened at the place where the river meets the sea." My chest was unbearably hot, and it was all I could do to prevent myself from tearing off my T-shirt and touching my breasts to soothe them. "That spot, that's where it happened."

Ferrera's smile shrank by just a notch. The gun was pointed down now, down at the bed, at my heart. "What happened?"

Chico jerked around in the chair, and it clattered against the floor. He let out a deep grunt of frustration.

I stood up, feeling heavy as cement, and tried to walk towards the balcony beyond the glass doors. I wanted the flurries of snow to cool my burning face and chest. Tied up as he was, it seemed that Chico was trying to drag the chair towards me, but I couldn't reach him, and instead fell on one knee. When I tried to get up, it was like a vine had lassoed my leg. This time I was going down whether I or anybody else wanted me to or not.

PART THREE

ONE
THE BODY IN THE WATER

She wasn't an initiate, but in her white dress she felt holy like one. She had built an altar on the beach in the early hours, piling offerings on a white sheet at the lonely spot where the river met the ocean. Purple bougainvillea, white lilies, a gold-bead necklace Alberto had given her, another necklace of green malachite beads, Florida water, coconuts and mangoes, little plastic mirrors. She pushed it all into the ocean chanting, "Madre de Agua, *tengo Kuta pa' usted. Aquí 'ta lo suyo. ¡Lléveselo y deme lo mío!*"

Then, so that Mama Chola would not be jealous, on an old yellow dress she grouped offerings for her: peacock feathers, plantain leaves dipped in honey, a bottle of white wine, a coral necklace and more little plastic-framed mirrors. The goddesses both loved mirrors.

She poured the wine and kept the bottle, and the offering sank immediately to the river's bottom and then rolled slowly out past the turquoise line of the delta to the ocean.

Aurora never liked to be indoors any more, unless she was fucking or being fucked. She had turned into a hotfooted whore, as the saying went. She walked barefoot on the sand by the river, humming a lullaby. "*A la nanita nana, nanita eha, nanita eha. Mi nena tiene sueño, bendito sea, bendito sea.*"

The river was all different colors, crystalline upstream, *nanita eha*, muddied green downstream, *nanita eha, nanita eha*. But where the river met the ocean, a deep blue ran, and beneath it there was a body of water that was a shade of turquoise that she loved. It was shaped like a woman. She had seen that womanly shape in the water many times.

It floated right at the surface of the water. So it couldn't be Madre de Agua, the ocean goddess. While voluptuous like Chola, the shape was too serene to be Chola, and also too bright a turquoise. *Nanita eha, nanita eha,* the body of a very delicious woman. Yes, there was a woman in the water, there where the river met the ocean and only she, Aurora, knew that it was neither the ocean goddess nor the river goddess, but a new entity. Mother, and mistress, and something else too: different robes, different rules, a goddess who walked a different path than Mother of Water, the sea tyrant and Chola, the tramp.

Yes, and who would know that Aurora wanted other things in her life, *nanita nana, nanita eha.* She didn't just want to follow the Chola path, which was really the *chocha* path, the wide open cunt that let herself be fucked and carried along by whoever was fucking her.

It was true, that had been her path. *Bendito sea.* But now that she had her daughter again, she wanted something different. Nobody would have guessed that she had other ideas in her head, or any ideas at all.

A body made for it, that was what Alberto said. Made for fucking.

Chico on the other hand had always taken her body for granted. But then again, things had been different with Chico. They had been young and naive together, struggling musician, patient wife. Poor as the zinc-roofed shacks they'd been born in. In hindsight, it was a bore. But at the time . . . yes, she had been happy at the time. Before the baby died.

You could say that it was Chico's fault she turned into a whore.

Some might say she had become the worst type of *puta,* a woman who would go with anybody and do anything. That was a lie. She had simply discovered that, after all, after his affair and her bitter rage over his betrayal, after all, she liked fucking when there was no love involved.

To admit that was to risk being called a *puta*. Now she did what she pleased.

The truth was that she'd been faithful to Alberto most of the time she'd been with him. She was more faithful than his wife! After all, she only fucked other women. He knew about it, and most of the time she let him watch. She was free in her body. As she liked to put it, she loved her body. Especially at times like this with the salt breeze blowing over the dunes, and all the different shades of green, yellow and blue she saw in land, sea and sky. Her body felt like the sand now. Like she was about to become a fluid being of sand and water and blood.

"*A la nanita nana, nanita nana . . .* "

After she passed the turquoise body in the river, she took off her rubber sandals and walked into the shallows. "*Nanita eha. Mi Alba tiene sueño, y yo también. Yo también.*"

She was tired. She wished she had the baby with her so that she could sleep with her on the simple cot in the shack with the ocean humming in their ears, the waves rocking them both steadily to sleep.

The tide was low, the water washed over her feet and ankles, and when it sucked the sand from under her feet, she felt a melting in her bones as if part of her was floating away. One moment she was standing there, feeling her feet squish into the wet sand, with the hot sun bearing down on her with its fierce bald eye. The next moment *she* was there: Isis, her glowing amber eyes devouring her thin face.

She used to hate Isis. Isis had destroyed her first life, the life of a trusting housewife.

Isis was just walking up to her now, almost exactly to the point where the river met the ocean. She knew then. She didn't have to look into her eyes to know. It was because of those golden, almost Arab, eyes, and that perfect body that Chico had wandered off right at the time their baby needed him.

Chico. In her first life, he was her ideal man: mulatto body, innocent heart. But he turned out to be a dog, just like most men. A very common kind of dog. *Perro realengo.* That's why she turned into a bitch. Different, at least from most of the women she knew.

And now she was staring into those beautiful yellow-green eyes, eyes too big for Isis' face. Isis had high cheekbones, naturally bee-stung lips and thick dark hair that she had stopped bleaching.

"Where is your child?" Isis said.

All that beauty gone to waste. The woman had no sense of herself beyond Alberto. Or Chico for that matter. Aurora scrutinized Isis' pregnant body and drawn face. She knew that Isis would do anything to protect her child, which judging from the height of her belly was a boy. Of course, that would make Alberto happy.

"What is it to you?"

He had no other children, except for her own girl, Alba. Alba Hilesca. The baby she had brought into being on purpose to replace the first child. Aurora couldn't blame Isis for taking her chance now, watching out for her own kid.

"I want to know what kind of mother you are," said Isis, stroking her high-pointed belly.

A lock of her own salt-drenched, kinky hair fell into Aurora's mouth, and she pulled it out. She was glad she hadn't brought the baby with her. She liked this desolate place, and the simple wooden house that had belonged to her grandmother Ana Mata; but for the baby it was dangerous.

"I left the baby in San Juan. I came to Loíza Aldea to bring offerings to the place where the river meets the sea. The water saints protect me."

Of course she wasn't about to tell this bitch that Mother of Water and Chola did whatever the hell they wanted. Sure, you could ask them for something, but that didn't mean that they'd give it to you.

She had come here to ask that she be allowed to be the kind of mother she had never had, and had never even heard about: a devoted mother, who neither abandoned nor abused her child. A mother like you saw only in church in the statue of the Virgin smiling down at her holy baby. And maybe the Virgin was only a good mother because the baby was so holy. She didn't know whether the *nkisis* were interested in her petition. Sometimes they were interested in good things, and sometimes they craved evil acts to feed their rage.

"So you're protected," said Isis. "How dumb to believe in such garbage."

"The day will come when you'll look for protection, too."

Isis blinked, and Aurora laughed. "What you really want scares you. That's why someday you'll want the *nkisis* to help you."

Sometimes you got what you wanted. Did that mean you were protected? Sometimes you didn't get shit, you got hurt bad. Aurora didn't care whether she was protected or not right now. Alba wasn't here, so nothing Isis did could faze her. Isis could kill her, true. Then Jahaira would take care of Alba. Jahaira was with Alba now, said she loved her like the daughter she never had. She could count on her sister. She wasn't like the cousins who had told her they'd take care of the baby a few times, and when she got to the building, she could hear the baby wailing. And when she went upstairs, she would find Alba alone, hungry, her diaper soaked with piss and shit.

"I'll pay you," said Isis. "I'll pay you anything to leave."

Aurora looked away. The figure underneath the water was rocking crazily in the tide. It never drifted away, though.

"Anything," Isis wrung her hands, her amber eyes liquid, her mouth loose and wet like a drug addict's. Alberto used to put Isis on drugs to pacify her, to keep her calm and happy, he told Aurora. But she knew he didn't want Isis to take any drugs, now that she was pregnant. Alberto loved Isis in his way. That's why Aurora had tried to love the bitch too.

"You don't understand. I am leaving. I'm just trying to keep it quiet. He doesn't want me to leave. He said I couldn't leave the island. He wants to set me up in my own apartment . . . " At this, Isis' nostrils flared and her eyes narrowed. "But I just want to get the hell away from this island."

Alberto said she didn't have to be his secretary, anymore. If she wanted to work, his family could get her any position she wanted. She could work on TV. The Ferreras controlled all the newspapers, television and radio stations, after all. He needed to fuck her. "Your body is made for this. It's made for me." She didn't question anything. She didn't want to be his wife, she didn't want to be any man's wife.

What she wanted most now was to be a different kind of woman for her daughter.

Isis' forehead got all creased, she squinted and then suddenly she started screaming. "¡*Animal, bruta, puta!* You're the one who won't leave him alone! You made Chico leave, and now you won't leave!"

Aurora put her hands on her hips. "You're not listening to me. You don't really know what you want, and that makes you crazy half the time. If you go on like this, you won't carry that baby to term."

Isis collapsed on her knees and started making choking and sobbing noises.

Aurora put her hands on her hips. "Who the hell are you to come here to the sacred spot where the river meets the sea and tell me what to do?"

Isis looked up, her pretty features swollen from crying. "So leave then! Leave now, if it's true you want to go."

Aurora laughed and licked her lips, like when she was a kid in the barrio and knew she was going to be hurt and she let loose with all her spite, the rage that usually she kept very deep inside, to make sure she hurt back as much as they hurt her. Like the three men who had taken her when she was fifteen. She stabbed two of them in the groin before the third one beat the shit out of her and nearly killed her. She didn't have time to ask Chola for anything, and Chola hadn't done anything for her then.

Then there had been that other time, right after she had stopped talking to Chico. She had poured honey for Chola in the river for five days straight, asking for a man she could make a deal with. She wanted a man who would give her a child and help with the child.

A week after that, she woke up one morning with the idea of seeking out Alberto Ferrera.

That very week, Ferrera took her to lunch at the Ritz Carlton in Isla Verde. They sat at a table overlooking the beach. He told her there was something "different" about her, putting his hand way up on her thigh under the table. He ordered "*cru*" this and that, French food that sounded exotic, but when it came to the table it was just underdone steak, french fries, barely cooked asparagus and a flan with a sugary crust.

"Let's be clear. You use me, I'll use you," she said.

Alberto's dark, hard eyes looked deeply into hers for the first time.

"I like that you're so direct. Who says love can't be like business?"

She put down the knife she'd used to cut the bloody meat. One bite and it had disgusted her. "I never said anything about love."

"Good." He had the perfectly white face and thin red lips of a vampire, and black hair she was sure that he dyed. He smiled without showing teeth. Not a passionate man, but Aurora had never expected that. Just somebody as strong as she was.

"I'm leaving, after Alberto gives me the next installment of my allowance. He thinks I'm using it for a house in Santa María, but actually I'm taking the money and running."

She observed the color rising in Isis' face again. "That's not the only time he's given me money."

"*¡Puta!*" Isis tried to get up and slap her, but Aurora stepped aside.

"You know, I can see it's a boy." It was funny the way Isis' hand stopped in mid-air. "You'll lose it, though, your blood is thin. You have no will. And you'll never have another one."

"Shut your shit-eating mouth! *¡Cállate! ¡Cállate ya!*" Isis lunged, grabbed a big handful of Aurora's hair and yanked at it.

Aurora fell to her feet.

"Shit-eating, cunt-licking *puta* from a long line of *putas*! *¡Cállate ya!*" Isis shrieked.

Aurora touched the burning spot on her scalp. When she saw the blood on her hand and felt blood trickling down to her lips, she licked them and sprang at Isis, pushing the taller woman and then punching her hard in the stomach.

"I said you wouldn't have this child, and you won't!" Aurora punched her again. Isis doubled over, grabbed at her stomach and started howling.

There was nobody on the beach. For all the allure of the spot where the river met the ocean, the beach itself was a place where criminals brought things to get rid of, bloodied bats, knives, clothes, occasionally a body. Nobody was going to hear the crazy bitch screaming like that.

"I like to fuck, but that don't mean I'm a *puta*!" snapped Aurora. "You don't like Alberto's dick, so that makes me a *puta*? You don't like your own cunt, the only thing you could do in the bed last time was suck my titties!"

In the bed, Isis had stared at her naked body, at her breasts. "They're too big, grotesque," she had said to Alberto, not addressing Aurora at all, as if Aurora couldn't understand what Isis and Alberto were saying.

Alberto, shameless as he was, told Isis. "You'll feel differently if you touch them. Go ahead and touch them."

Aurora lay there, her body a feast for Isis' eyes and fingers, and Alberto's eager cock.

She liked to open her legs and show them her meaty pussy, shaven so that every glistening purple fold was visible.

At first it seemed as if she was simply the passive recipient of Isis' tremulous cat licks and of the urgent state of Alberto's penis, which he offered to her mouth first before dipping slowly into Aurora.

She would pull away and then take his glistening cock in her hand and make Isis lick the pussy juice off it.

Aurora was always in control. This particular type of control excited her so much that her consciousness flew up somewhere to the top of the bedroom ceiling, from where she stared down at the scene below, gazed down at herself open and generous, stroking Alberto as he entered her and guiding Isis' tongue as it flicked at Alberto's cock.

Now Aurora tore at the low bodice of the loose white dress and exposed her full breasts with the purple nipples, the breasts that Alberto and Isis both considered grotesque and out of proportion, and yet never stopped fondling once they had them naked and available.

She offered a breast to Isis. "*¡Chupa, nenita!* You've done it before, but now there's milk. I have enough milk for you and my daughter. Maybe both of you will grow up to be good girls!"

Isis stood up, now sobbing quietly. "You want to kill my child?"

"*A la nanita nana, nanita eha, nanita eha, Mi nena tiene sueño, y yo también,*" Aurora sang, thinking that Isis really was as helpless as her own baby. "Let's go take a nap in the shack, Isis, and I'll let you suck my *tetas* the way you like."

Then it started to happen. What she had known in her heart, yes, because when she saw Isis there at the point where the river met the ocean, she had known what would happen. Although she hadn't expected it at this precise moment, nor in this particular way.

He appeared from behind the mangrove trees, looking like the devil and holding what looked like a Beretta.

"You bitch. You dare try to kill my child? It's bad enough that you were going to run off without telling me. But you try to kill my son?"

She barely hesitated. "I can leave whenever I want. And there's nothing but a mongoloid retard in that belly."

She never knew why she couldn't lie, even to save her life. Why not tell him she was jealous and upset? Alberto knew her, and he wouldn't have believed it, anyway. She hadn't planned on it, but as soon as it all started happening, she had meant to beat the baby out of Isis' stomach.

It was beyond words. Just as she had known as soon as she saw Isis that she was going to die. She didn't know Alberto had been listening to them all along. She didn't hear the shot, but the impact made her stumble, and then she fell on her back into the water.

The only sensation at first was that her head felt heavy, her neck stiff. For a moment she imagined that her head was a coconut, an offering to that shape in the water.

Isis was standing over her, with a hand to her mouth. She made a sound that was a giggling gasp. "Oh, no. Oh, no."

With a supreme effort, Aurora lifted her head out of the water, caught her breath and then hissed at Alberto, "Your son won't live. My daughter will be your only heir."

Isis started to rock her whole body, but she didn't make a sound now.

"You can't know that," Alberto said to Aurora, and he shot her again, this time in the upper right corner of her chest, close to her armpit.

Flamboyán flowers bloomed in the water. She wasn't looking up at them anymore. She was looking down at them, and she could see now that her own body was falling deeper into the water, past the Flamboyant flowers and into the turquoise shape.

She realized suddenly that it was the shadow of her own body that she had been seeing all along! Her body! She would become an *nkisi*, a goddess different from Chola and the Mother of the Waters. And just as important. Her body started to drift away becoming as she had always wanted: sand and sea and blood.

Isis was yelling at Alberto. "I didn't want her dead. I only wanted to teach her a lesson."

Alberto leapt into the water and grasped Aurora's body by an ankle, trying to tear it away from the turquoise shape. The turquoise shadow in the water reached out long, loving arms to her. But Alberto tore her away from that lovely embrace. He grabbed hold of Aurora's legs before she could float away. He dragged the body, bringing it to the shore. The white shift was soaked in swirls of red.

They wrapped her in sheets that they found in her own shack, the shack that had belonged to her grandmother, Ana Mata. Alberto put his hand over her eyelids and tried to close them, but when he brought his hand away, he saw that the lids had closed only half way. Then they put her body, the left leg dangling longer than the right, in the trunk of Isis' Mercedes Benz. The trunk held a shovel, cans, matches, rags, garbage bags and newspapers.

Aurora was almost clear of her body now, staring at the livid skin, the gnarled fingers and the dress spattered in a pattern of flamboyant flowers. But she couldn't leave it.

They drove away to a forest in the Toro Negro mountains, honeycombed with caves.

Isis stood a few feet away while Alberto dug a shallow grave. When he was done, he rolled the body into the ditch. Isis squeezed fluid from one of the cans over the body, and threw a match on it, but the fire would not light. She threw match after match. Finally the fire started its devouring rhythm.

She watched the skin on her own face shiver and move as if black letters were crawling across it. She even managed to make the charred hands pop up in the air.

Isis screamed. And yet, Aurora, could not feel the pain! She was stuck somewhere far away from the water. They had cheated her of her fate as a water *nkisi*.

Then the man and woman shoveled dirt over the remains. Smoke seeped upward. There was nothing now that would cool this fire. She was tied to the bones like a ragged scarf unfurled from its owner's neck, blowing in the breeze, fluttering over them. She who had loved the sun and the sea was now hurtled into darkness so profound that she began the long forgetting of the body. Then she was part of the darkness itself, the darkness whistling through the forest on the mountain, where her spirit wandered.

TWO

THE QUEEN OF THE SLUMS

A t the place where the river met the sea, black rocks separated the dark blue ocean depths from the green river. Even as I opened my eyes, I could still smell the iron. Sea water. Blood.

As I tried to adjust my mind to the real world, I saw a snowy dusk. There was a metallic taste on my tongue, like I'd been sick or drunk. It felt like thick heavy sleep was still holding its arms out to me, waiting for me to fall back into them.

The bedroom light was off, and evening was coming on: cobalt with pink-banked clouds. I could see the balcony with its black ironwork, refracted by the glass of the French doors.

I sat up, then turned my head and gasped. Ferrera and Alba were sitting on the settee just watching me, their faces practically glowing in the half-light.

Chico was still tied up in the chair. He was strangely silent, like something really important had just been said. Now he was trying to stare Ferrera down, but Ferrera was ignoring him.

"You passed out," said Ferrera to me. "You were in a trance, were you not?"

I put a hand to my hair, which was wet, and started to respond, but he didn't let me.

"You sweated to a degree I have never witnessed before. Your eyes were open, but you didn't speak. We thought you were dead at first. Do you remember anything?"

I remembered as I looked at him. "I saw what happened between Aurora and you and Isis." I touched my T-shirt. The cloth was soaked through, like I'd been swimming.

I said breathlessly, "At the place where the river meets the ocean, Isis ordered Aurora to leave the island." I paused. "Aurora attacked Isis. You shot Aurora. You killed her."

Alba stood up from the settee, and came over to me. "You saw what?" Her eyes had the glittering dilated look again.

I nodded. "Isis was pregnant, and Aurora attacked her." I glanced at Ferrera.

He stood up from the settee, hands in the pockets of his smoking jacket, the butt of his gun just visible. There was a smile, a fucking calm smile on his face.

"My dear Fina, you had, shall we say, a vision. My dear, you are very gifted with *percepciones*, as we say on the island. But just because you have these, these visions, does not mean they are true."

My visions. Now that I had found them, now that I had discovered that other world I always knew was there waiting for me, it was hard to describe it to others.

I closed my eyes, frustrated, and then opened them. "Okay, so you tell me what happened?"

"My dear, that's my point. I wasn't there. I don't know what happened. I don't even know if there is a place where the river meets the ocean. Do you? Have you been there?"

I opened my mouth and then closed it. In my dream, in my "vision," as he put it, wild tall waves broke over the rocks and melted into a slow green river.

"I'm sure it exists. In Puerto Rico, somewhere." And then I remembered, "At the house of Ana Mata. The Mata house." I looked at Alba. I'd never seen the kid so still and focused. "Alba, I think we may be distant relatives."

But Ferrera wasn't having any of it, and I had to hand it to him, not once had he lost his temper. "But my dear, can you really launch an accusation based on something you've never seen?"

He didn't need his gun. He could and would defeat me by logic alone.

I blinked a few times. "Well, you're right if you look at it from that perspective. But that's not the perspective I was looking at it from. I saw what happened. I saw the place."

Chico shook himself in the chair so that it bumped against the floor. "There is a place like that," he said. "You know about it." He shot Ferrera a sharp look. "It's where the Río Grande de Loíza meets the sea. And in fact Aurora's family had a house there." He looked down. "Fina, you're right! Aurora's grandmother was named Ana Mata. The house on the beach belonged to her."

"A house?" Ferrera grinned and shook his head. "A shack with a zinc roof is a house?"

Alba turned her head and said quietly, "So you have seen the place?"

"Yes, for goodness sake's yes, I have seen a place in Puerto Rico where ocean meets river," Ferrera confessed. "There are many places like that there. Let's not forget we are talking about an island. But the point is that because somebody sees something in a so-called 'vision,' it doesn't mean that it happened. People see things in their dreams to suit their psychological needs. People dream about things they have never seen in real life, and never could see."

"Papi, you went to that place? That place where Mami's family had a house?" Alba's voice was suddenly tinny like that of a much younger child.

"It wasn't a house." Ferrera came over to Alba and put his arms around her. "A house is what you're going to live in when we go back to Puerto Rico. A house that was built like a fortress. And a plantation house. A house with countless balconies. The house of lineage. Of a dynasty."

Alba snuggled close to her father, and planted a smackeroo right on his nose. "And now that you've signed the papers, I am the heiress." She kept on kissing him all over his face, with her arms wrapped around his thick velvet-clad body. Finally she planted a big wet one on his lips.

I tried to keep the distaste out of my expression, since Ferrera still had the gun in his pocket. And really, who knew what exactly might offend famously inbred aristocrats from Puerto Rico? But Ferrera beamed at Alba.

She was his spitting image: Ivory soap skin, shark eyes, that almost Asian black hair.

"You can ask Miss Fina to come visit you if you like," he said to Alba.

He looked at me. "We can continue these fascinating conversations about perception and reality. I am quite interested in the paranormal, Miss Fina. I would like to hear more about what happens to you when you go into these trances."

"I haven't had that much experience with them," I said, biting my lip. "And it's called being *montada*. Not a trance."

I hate to admit that I was actually a little flattered. He thought I was fascinating? Was he making a play at me? No, obviously, he was just manipulating me. But he seemed so . . . friendly. And he himself was interesting.

Shit, evil wasn't obvious at all, at least not all the time. I could see why Aurora and Isis had been drawn to him as much as to Chico.

"*Montada*, yes, yes, of course. Aurora used to talk like that, too. You and Alba can both go out to the house near the Río Grande de Loíza, and explore it."

"Explore it?" Alba crooked an eyebrow. "The shack? The shack you said at first you didn't know anything about."

She easily pulled out Ferrera's gun from the smoking jacket pocket and pointed it at him.

I have to hand it to the guy. Even that didn't faze him. He grinned at his daughter, whose skin had gotten, unbelievably, even whiter. "I am glad that Isis' baby died. You are exactly like me. You are the child that I was meant to have."

He was sweet-talking her, sure. But I believed him. Alba may have lacked Ferrera's finesse, since she didn't grow up with all the guy's access. But they were both clearly cut from the same glacier—anybody could see that. And you could tell it made Ferrera teary proud.

But his sweet talk was one thing, and his instinct for survival something else. He made a quick grab for the gun.

Alba stepped back. "You never came to get me. To see me. In those slums where I lived with Titi Jahaira. Llorens Torres, then Coop City. All those years."

"My dear, I came looking for you just a few months ago. Didn't I? Only now did I allow Isis to finally leave me. That was the deal: she would finally go find Chico. That was, as it were, in exchange for my getting to keep you. Years ago, Isis just wouldn't have . . . "

"Liar! Like you stopped from doing whatever the fuck you wanted! You told me Isis killed Mami so I would hurt her. You didn't want to do it yourself. But you know what, motherfucker? It's like you said: *La sangre llama.*" Legs planted wide apart and braced for the recoil, Alba shot him.

He stumbled down on his knees and he held out both his arms to her. On one hand his finger was pointed as if he was about to say something. He tried, but all he could do was smile, cough, smile. He was still smiling, still bent on persuading her, persuading us all.

Then she shot him a second time, in the mouth; his smile widened into an expression of happiness, even as the blood streamed out. His body finally collapsed.

She looked down at him on the floor. "Fool. I wasn't asking no question."

She wiped the gun off on her silk shirt and went to Chico. "Hold it in your hands!"

"Alba . . . "

"Do it, or I'll shoot you now! Fuck this shit!" She took a knife, a little paring knife, out of her skirt pocket and held it to Chico's throat. "Gonna bleed you like a goat if you don't do it."

Chico took the gun and held it gingerly.

"Hold tight with your fingers."

Alba took the gun out of his hands and placed it next to the door. Then she sprinted out of the room, the little paring knife still in one hand.

I bounded over to Chico and started to untie him.

He shouted at me, "You can catch her, Fina. Tackle her! She put the gasoline in the bottle and took it back to Perla's store. She killed my Isis! My poor, sweet, Isis."

I ran after her then. Not because I wanted to catch a killer. Not because I wanted to spend more time with my only possible remaining relative in the world. I just wanted to get away from the truth in his voice.

THREE

THE GOLDEN DRAGON

On the way to get Chico at the 24th Precinct, I noticed that the snowfall from the day Ferrera went *sayonara* had turned into big puddles of dirty slurp. Chico had been held up for questioning for several days, but in the end, that cop Marino believed my story when the forensics evidence backed it. The way Chico's prints came out on the gun wasn't consistent with the shooting angle. The NYPD put out search alerts for Alba.

I was standing on the sidewalk in front of the 24th Precinct, looking studiously down at my feet, when somebody said, "Hey, there, you waiting for de León?"

I looked up, all the way up, and nodded.

Marino was fucking tall. And he had strangely dark eyes for such a fair-haired type. Really dark gray, kind of nice I guess. When I'd been zonked out at the hospital, I'd only really seen him out of the corner of my eye. He hooked a couple fingers through his belt loop. He was wearing a real ugly-ass jacket, plaid, like detective garb cliché. He coughed suddenly, a real in your face raca raca raca type of cough.

"He your type?" Marino asked.

Just then, I saw Chico exiting the first glass door, all hollow-eyed and grim. I put out a hand to shake. "Detective, I am so grateful for all your work on the case. I am really impressed."

"You impress easy. We ain't even caught the criminal." His smile was surprisingly shy. "You know, I was wondering about all this magic stuff. I was wondering if you'd like to tell me more about it?"

"Sure, Detective, I can talk to you about *Palo*. Maybe it would help with understanding Alba's motives."

"Actually . . . "

Chico appeared next to Marino and nodded at him, then turned to me. "I need to go home to change. Some guy vomited on me last night." Chico's silk shirt reeked of vomit and sweat, even urine. There were basset hound pouches under his eyes and a three-day's growth of silvery beard that made him look ten years older.

"Well, I have your number," said Marino.

I nodded, and reached over to peck Chico on the cheek, but homeboy didn't return the favor.

"Let's just walk," he said, heading west towards Amsterdam so fast I had to trot to catch up.

"I bought you rice and beans and chicken from Los Compadres." I held out a big paper bag.

"You shouldn't have troubled yourself." He didn't slow down or even look me in the eye.

"*Mijo*, what is it?"

"Nothing."

"Why are you being so uppity? If it wasn't for me, you'd still be in the slammer."

He turned on a sharp angle, and we stopped right in the middle of Amsterdam Avenue. A kid in baggy jeans and a do-rag bumped into him and cursed us out, but Chico ignored him.

He pressed his face close to mine. "What?"

"You heard me. You . . . "

"Tell me one thing?" He took a breath, and I nodded. "Why the hell didn't you lickety split it after the demon child?"

"What?" I licked my lips nervously. Maybe it was for the wrong reason, but I had run like the fucking wind. "You think I didn't catch up to her on purpose?"

"Fina, or shall I say 'Miss Fina'?" I blushed at his reference to Ferrera.

"Look at you." He grabbed my arm and looked up and down my body in a real nasty way. "You've lost some weight, lately, but you can still tackle just about anybody in one jump. Especially if they're 4 feet 10 inches and weigh 85 pounds. If you'd bothered doing what you do best, I wouldn't have spent one minute in the slammer."

I handed him the brown bag, which was letting out the delicious greasy aroma of Dominican *chicharrones*. "Here's the food. Enjoy, and see you later."

He took the bag with one hand. With the other, he grabbed me by the arm, jerking me back, or trying to. "Why? Just tell me why you let her go."

"I used to think she was a bad seed, too." I blinked. It wasn't until I answered him that I realized what I felt about Alba. "I think I understand what drives her. Her parents disappeared, and she didn't know what the hell happened. Then her father showed up and said he loved her, and he kind of did, but he was such a fucking liar, he hurt her. Again. And she can't stand to be hurt anymore." My eyes started to water. "I can really understand that."

"Really?" He let go of me. "You think she's the only abandoned child in the ghetto? Well, you know what? I can't understand you." He threw down the brown bag with the Dominican food. Liquid started to seep through one side of it.

I didn't bother picking it up.

When I got home, my phone was ringing off the hook.

"Fina." Victor's gravelly voice.

I sniveled.

"What's wrong?" His voice went from husky to oily. "You want me to come over?"

"No." I started to tear up real bad. Fuck it. Chico was right. Was it Alba I felt bad for, or just myself? "I need to step in now, Victor. I need it really bad."

I took Victor's series of grunts for understanding, and I stopped my sniveling.

"I been looking for this Alba scum," said Victor, and I realized that his oil-smooth voice was more dangerous than the gravelly one. "I think we should flush her out by having a ceremony to bury the bones in Central Park. I think she's still in the city. She wants those bones, Fina."

I didn't ask him how he knew she was still in the city. He had his ways. Maybe he had sent out his *nkuyo* and *nfuiri* messengers for looking and seeing, like the Ancient One. Or he had used more mundane messengers like Niño.

I had never known much about my mother because she died when I was born. For the short time she had taken care of Alba, Aurora had tried to protect her kid. She'd done more for Alba in the short time she'd been with her than Ferrera ever had.

"If I was Alba, and that was all that was left of my mother, I'd want them bones, too," I said to Victor.

Victor grunted.

Then I thought of the fedora that Alba was wearing on the night she'd sung Chico's song, and I added hastily, "I don't want to forget about Genio."

Victor was plenty mad, I could tell now. Finally, in a voice as quiet as snow, he said, "The first week of March isn't so far away. When this icedown melts, we are taking the bones to Central Park and burying the *nfuiri* in an anthill."

Before I could say anything else, he hung up on me.

Victor had a kind of understated ferocity that reminded me of my father, of the strength I always knew was in him. But my father had been gentle, too. The way Chico was always touching people with his hands reminded me of my father's gentle hands. I thought one was my mentor, and the other more than a friend. But now I had to conclude that both these guys just let me fit into their own fucking agendas at random. They froze me out when I showed what I'd been hiding under my ghetto tough-girl ways.

Damn them.

I stepped in. I focused on my father's eyes on the night of the storm, fierce eyes that softened, even though he knew he was leaving me. Maybe because he was leaving me. Maybe he was just one more ghetto father, carelessly making babies all over the place and crying a little over them right before he went on to ruin the next life.

"*Nfuiri*, if you take me to him, I'll do what you want, even if it means taking the bones to your daughter, and having Victor and all the *nkisis* come after me."

I was floating over the trees, the hundreds of trees. It was a park that was northwards, no lamps.

The monastery, the monastery from before.

The buildings crowded together, a red banner painted intricately with a dragon. A golden dragon.

At the copy shop on Broadway and 108th St., I surfed the net, looking for monasteries in Manhattan, but I couldn't find any near a big park.

There was a convent in Queens; there was a Dominican order monastery upstate. When I stepped in, I'd seen that the buildings were built close together, and I knew because of that the place was somewhere way uptown. Washington Heights, Inwood, somewhere like that.

A link came up: GO MEDIEVAL IN MANHATTAN AT THE CLOISTERS.

I looked at the pictures. It was the place I had seen when I stepped in on the day of Isis' death.

At 190th St. I knew I was close. The brick buildings were clustered together, which gave them a kind of glowering, pissed-off look. From the corner MTA station, I could see the evergreen lushness of Fort Tryon Park. But the only Chinese restaurant I saw was called The Lucky Spoon.

At 191st St., I saw a sign for a 99-cent store that said Banzai. Japanese, but I decided to go in anyway.

A big tapestry hung over the cash register. Burgundy background, embroidered with the image of a big yellow fire-breathing dragon. A woman was reading a newspaper under the picture. She had that dyed orangey hair Latinas for some reason love.

I went up to her, but she didn't budge from her reading.

"Did this place used to be called 'The Golden Dragon'?"

"Nah." She flipped a page and didn't bother looking up.

"What about that picture?"

She looked up real annoyed, but when she got a good look at me, she shot up straight. She was in her fifties, and I could see the little gray hairs sticking out from her widow's peak. Her skin was light brown.

"My voice ain't anything like me, right?"

She got all giggly on me. "I'm the golden dragon. That's a *thangka* I bought to fit my nickname." She jerked her head at the tapestry.

I nodded, and she pointed at her hair and eyes. "You know, golden."

Her hair, like I said, was dyed that dryish orangey color, and her eyes were brown like most people's.

She laughed at my expression. "You so polite, *mija*. I just kidding you. I got nicknamed the Golden Dragon 'cause a my temper. When I'm on a bend, I'm like a fire-breather."

"Do you know if Andrés Mata lives around here? Or used to?"

She looked surprised, then looked into my eyes and said sharply. "What you want to know?"

So I told her about the last night I saw my father. I even told her about the dog hanging from the tree. It was one of those moments. She got emotional because, yes, she knew Andrés Mata very well. She blubbered at first and then went into a loud bawling fit right there in the 99-cent store. When a real customer popped in at that moment, she brought the pitch to a hysterical high and actually chased the teenager out of the store. When she came back in, she locked the door and started to calm down.

I asked, "Is he in jail?"

She came back to the cash register, and grabbed my hand. "They strung that dog up there and choked it slowly as a warning to your papi. They wanted him to know that was what they'd do to him if he stuck around. They blamed everything on him. They knew he was a real powerful *palero*, but every time something bad happened, they blamed it on him."

I nodded. "Abuela told me that was why he left. He was a *brujo*, and everyone hated him."

Caterina's eyes blazed, for it was Caterina, my father's girlfriend from when I was a kid. "Your grandmother, she was one of them."

"She wanted him out of there?"

She looked at me long and hard. "*Mija*, do you really want to know what happened? You really want to hear this shit? It happened so long ago and maybe it's best for you, *mija*, not to hear all the details."

I paused. I knew something bad was coming, and part of me didn't want to hear it. But it was inevitable that I learn what it was, because in a sense, I already knew it. "It's something I've been needing to remember my whole life."

She nodded. "That night? The night of the hurricane. They strung your papi up that night. They hung him like they did the dog. Then they took the body and they buried it somewhere. I don't know where."

I stared at her. "They hung him from the mango tree?"

"It was people I knew from always: the *colmado*, the horse races, from around the corner."

I looked down. I couldn't visualize it, my father hanging, hanging like a dog from the mango tree. His eyes bulging, his tongue swollen. I looked up. Those details I didn't want to hear.

"How . . . "

Caterina took both my hands in hers. "It was fast. It happened fast."

She had tried to push through that crowd, but they wouldn't let her. His body shook, it shook all over, but when she got to the tree and grabbed my father's legs, he wasn't shaking anymore.

"And when I kind of leaned over and just held his legs in my arms, that's when I knew it wasn't just rain on my face. You know what it was? Rocks. They started stoning me, and I was bleeding. I couldn't even feel the stones. Because of the storm and the shock. But I heard what they was saying: 'Kill her, kill the *puta*. She's a *bruja*, too, and a *puta*.'"

I heard a cry, a low continuous moan getting gradually higher, and when I realized that it was coming from somewhere in my twisted gut, I cried out loudly, striking the wood counter hard with both my fists, over and over again, until my hands started to bleed on the newly healed burns. I reeled away from the counter wondering where they'd buried him and if my grandmother had gone to the burial.

Caterina ran to slide a chair under me. She hugged me close, and I sobbed and blubbered until my head ached and the snot ran from my nose.

"What else?" I wiped part of my face carelessly with my T-shirt.

"I left later that night, like we was supposed to. But I left on my own."

The braying sound of my grief came back, and this time it sounded even stranger, like somebody grunting and moaning behind a door, and getting louder and darker, hairy and ugly, a monstrous howling animal with gnashing teeth, an image of what was inside me. It wasn't just my loss that was the monster. I was guilty.

"He was supposed to leave that night. The night of the hurricane. I thought I heard voices. He stayed until I fell asleep. He stayed for me."

I had known it. I had known it so many years ago, but had chosen to forget. "I got sick with dengue. And after that I couldn't remember."

"It was for the best. It was no use to you. What's the point of remembering something like that? Believe me, I wish I could forget it. I tried to forget when I came here. Drugs, you know. Finally over that shit. But I never forgot."

The hurricane, the rain that came down like a firing squad on the zinc roof. Did the rain cover over their voices? The shouts. The executioners. "Do you know their names?"

She looked away. "*Mija*, most of those people are gone or dead."

"Do you have anything? Anything of his?"

She hesitated. I could tell that, whatever it was, she wanted it for herself.

"I got it at home. Upstairs. You wanna wait on me?"

I walked around her store, thinking of the hurricane. They were going to leave Barrio Sal Pa' Fuera that night. But I woke up crying. The hurricane scared me. I called for him.

He didn't want to leave me at all. I thought he had left, but the irony is that he ended up dead because he decided not to leave. He never left me, never left Puerto Rico. Never.

All the bowls in Caterina's store were ceramic with blue and red Asian flower designs. There were bamboo trays and lacquer boxes. I opened the red and black lid of an oval box. There was a whole section with back scratchers, massage handles, foot massagers and musical hand balls. Every time I touched something, I tried to remember a detail about my father.

I remembered, he came into my room. His fierce eyes softened. I could always make that pleat between his eyebrows disappear. I caught his face suddenly. The scorpion eyes watching me as I held onto his fingers and fell back to sleep. He had stayed for me.

I was wondering if he had had a moustache. I just couldn't remember.

Caterina opened the back door of the store. She had a few pictures in her hand, and a big green plastic bag.

In the pictures: Caterina and my father. I had forgotten his flat, sweet nose. He didn't have a moustache in these pictures. His hair was curly, his lips pulpy. He had a manly bearing, but a very sweet face. He was tall, a good head and a half taller than

Caterina. In one of the pictures he was looking down at her and smiling. In another, he looked straight at the camera. The red-haired Caterina—real red hair in the pictures, not orange dye—wearing too much lipstick and eye makeup, looked up at him.

I looked at Caterina. I started to mumble something.

She said, "These things are for you, *mija*."

She opened the bag, and I peeked in: a familiar smell of leaves and dirt hit me. My heart beat fast. "How . . . "

"It's not what you think. It's like I told you. I don't know where . . . where they buried him. This is from his most important *nganga*."

Of course! He was a *palero*. Bones from one of his cauldrons.

She held the bag close to her body, like she wasn't totally psyched about handing it over.

"His *Palo* name was Tata Andrés Entierra Mundo. And all that was left of his tiny barrio *munanso* were the bones of his grandfather Ángel Mata." She twisted her mouth. "Your great-grandfather." She sighed and held out the bag to me.

I accepted it and thought of my vision of Aurora at the place where the river met the sea. "Who was Ana Mata?"

Caterina cocked her head. "I remember the name, but it's been a long time. Why do you ask?"

"I think I met a descendant of Ana Mata's, and I think we're related."

Caterina returned to her original position behind the glass counter and leaned over on her elbows. "That's good if you can find some family after all this time. I just know that your papi said the Matas broke up at the time of the great pandemic. That was after the occupation. Your papi, he was big on his family history. But I can't remember much of it. I barely know my own family. But I'm almost sure that Ana Mata was Ángel Mata's daughter."

You know how it is when a situation between neighbors or friends is as stiff as a turd? Lots of looking away when you pass each other on the steps. Efforts to do laundry at different times. If you're crazy, you might think of smearing dog crap on the asshole's door. I thought of that, but just like my fat girl avatar was giving way gradually to hell-if-I-knew what, my tendency to hit first and talk later was turning into a craving for talk for its own useless sake.

After I heard him dragging his cases up the stairs, I just barreled up there one night in late February and pounded hard on his door until he answered.

Hello, Fina, hello, Chico, how are you, Fina, how are you, Chico—like characters from some fucking lame-ass British drama series on PBS. He was still wearing a tuxedo from his gig. He was growing a moustache now, a bushy thing that covered half of his top lip. That seemed significant.

"Look," I said, and I started to flush in that unattractive way that seemed like my new thing. "I just want to say this: If I'd known you really loved Isis, I wouldn't have fed my crush. I just thought it was all about her being so, you know . . . " I paused. He was now looking me in the eyes at least. "So high society. I thought you had all this regret about your wife. That you loved Aurora. That you made a mistake."

"Just come in." He loosened his bow tie. He gestured at the futon frame sofa, and I sat down.

He took off the tuxedo jacket, flung it on the floor and sat down on the other end of the sofa. "Neither one of them understood how I felt. But Isis, you know, she played it safe. Staying with Ferrera, trying to give him his heir. I guess Aurora decided to seduce Ferrera to get back at me. Isis decided to stay with her husband for all those years."

He turned his face to me. His eyes were filled with liquid, and he brought up a hand to partly shield them: "This is the thing: I loved them both. In different ways, but strong. And always."

FOUR

GREEN THINGS

March came in PMS-ing, hot air streaked with icy winds. Fog floated up from the waters of Central Park and rested in the tree branches. My face and hands were soft from the haze. I could smell green things in the air.

One day, after sundown, Victor dragged me to the park to bury the bones. I brought the contents of the cauldron in one green plastic bag. I brought the other one too, the one that Caterina gave me. I hadn't completely accepted the story she told me about my father, but I didn't really know what to do with that bag of bone splinters and dirt that was supposed to be my ancestor Ángel Mata.

Victor found a spot on a hill filled with trees and brush in Central Park, near 106th St. He said there was an anthill there for three seasons of the year. To end a cauldron spirit, you place the *kiyumba*, or skull, in an anthill. The ants recognize the *nfuiri* and chew up the bones right away.

We had shovels and we took turns digging up earth. After twenty minutes, my arms gave out.

I stopped shoveling. "I don't see no ants."

With the fog that was wrapping around our hands and faces, we weren't seeing much of anything.

Victor scrunched up his forehead. He put the *nganga* earth, the charred half skull, and the splintered bones, in the shallow pit.

Besides the plastic bags with the bones and dirt, we had a lot of paper bags filled with what we needed.

He took a bell out of one of the bags, and rang it three times.

"*Nsambia arriba, Nsambia abajo, Nsambia por los cuatro costados. Nsambia* on all four sides. And in the middle, the *nganga nfuiri*. The cauldron is a symbol of the world," he said.

He brought out a rooster from another bag, firmly grasping its legs in one hand and holding its neck with the other in a way that calmed it.

"The *ngangulero* dominates the world of the cauldron," he continued. "The *palos* are the forest. The water is the river and the ocean. The *kiyumba*, bones and dirt from the tomb, are the cemetery. There are stones that hold the energy of the sun, the moon and the stars."

"That's what *paleros* do. For good and also, when necessary, for evil," I chimed in.

"Today we are going to destroy the world." Victor's voice got deeper, and he brandished his ancient *munanso* knife. He cleaved the rooster's throat so quickly, the animal didn't make a sound. He let the blood run into the earth of what had been the cauldron.

"Now she is in the earth." He took a swig from a bottle of rum, swished it around his mouth and spit the liquid onto the earth pit. Then he lit a cigar and put the lit end in his mouth. After a few seconds, he puffed out a few circles of smoke that blew away like feathers in the air.

I knelt next to the earth pit. "*Take me to the water.*" I closed my eyes.

My father was kneeling next to me by the river.

I touched the *morivivi* plant, and the purple leaves of the plant closed magically. I rubbed the leaves, but they were tightly furled. "It's dead."

"Only for a while. It dies to live again."

He closed his hand over mine. "Take my bones to the water after I die, and my spirit will become a god."

"Like Jesus?"

He shook his head. "An *nkisi*, a god of water and woods. Part of me will come back like the *morivivi*."

My voice was high, "But the *morivivi's* leaves are still closed."

He smiled, and all the lines of care vanished from his face. "You have to be patient. The spirit dies and is renewed. Eventually, the leaves will open again."

I got up. "*Take me to the water.*"

Water, a concentrated but narrow line of it, showered over my head and hands. My hands looked like I'd rubbed baby oil on them.

I waved my glistening hands at Victor. "Do you see?"

Then it started to rain, all over the gray cloud-banked sky as far as I could tell, all over the ground.

"That's our sign," Victor said. "Water. Fire to start the *nfuiri's* life, water to end it."

"Water's a strange sign to end life," I said.

Victor paid no attention to me, and started shoveling earth over the *nfuiri* bones and *palos*.

"Stop, Victor." I got down on my hands and knees and started scooping out dirt with my bare hands. I could smell green in the dirt, the green things the strange March heat was coaxing out of the earth. I pulled out the half skull and bones, crusty with dirt, and carefully put them back into one of the plastic bags.

"Fina, what the hell are you doing?"

I heard something and stopped digging. A couple holding jackets over their forearms walked past us. Because of the fog, I couldn't see their expressions, and they could barely see us.

"Fina, throw the dirt back!"

"Earth is flesh of the dead, their ground up bodies."

"Stand up, Fina!"

I brought some dirt up to my mouth and tasted it—gritty and strong with minerals. I wrinkled my nose, wondering if there were worms in the dirt, but I ate a handful of it anyway, and then another. It didn't go down easy, but the grass parts were refreshing.

"Mmm. The dead—the old order. Delicious."

When I looked up, Victor was examining me. "You know I know that you're not *montada*."

I swallowed the rest of the dirt, which passed down in a big choking clump. "I don't have to be. I know. I know that the bones have to go to the water."

Night deepened its shades of blue and purple. As we passed the Victorian lamps, they flickered on, one after another, looking like large fantastic fireflies in the fog.

"You can throw it all in the water, but I never heard of such a thing. I never done it, and I don't know the ritual for it. That hasn't been passed down. That hasn't been written." Victor walked over to a bench by the pool, put a hand on the back of the bench and closed his eyes.

In the silence of the trees I sensed another presence. If I gave the *nfuiri* up, I might never again be able to hear those voices, that other world. A tree branch cracked: tarit, tarit. *Rita.*" Well, Aurora was one thing, Rita was another. I didn't want Rita again.

"Aurora, come to me in the silence behind the silence, with the trees, with you."

A gust of wind blew over the trees at the edge of the half-frozen pool. *In the water. It dies to live again.*

"Where?"

"Right here," said a familiar voice.

I could barely see her because of the darkness and the haze. I heard Victor move. "We thought you might show up," he said flatly.

"I've been coming. For days now," said Alba. "You *paleros* take your fucking time, don't you?" Her voice caught, but then a few racking coughs left her choking for air.

"Are you okay, Alba? Are you sick?" I wondered if she had a gun on her.

She came closer. "Like you give a shit." Her voice was hoarse.

I glimpsed her limp hair, jeans, sweater, some kind of dark jacket. And now I could smell the rankness of dirty clothes, sweat, rum and a metallic nastiness . . . like she had a wound in her mouth.

A light came on suddenly from a flashlight she had turned on near my eyes and I covered them with my hands until she lowered the light. My head started to ache.

Her eyes were like holes. When you first looked into them, they seemed calm and empty, as if there was nothing there, as if she wasn't really there.

"I see you for what you are. I like the fact that you don't pretend to be a good girl."

"That's 'cause we family, girl, huh? Aurora's my mother . . . and you're what?"

"I think my great-grandfather was your great-grandmother's father."

"Wow, I can really see that," she snickered. "I don't know what 'family' means. I think we know that by now. Now that dear Papi ain't no more."

"Well, it's not your fault."

"You too goody-goody now, girl. What's the use of being big if you ain't bad?"

"What's the point of being bad if you're such a half-pint?" I tried to grab her, but she ducked me. "Stomp you out like an ant."

She darted in front of me so that I saw her rubber knob eyes and dark lips, and then she moved back, and then further away so that now she was just a voice in the fog. "Ant too fast for elephant." Her laughter was tinny like little bells in the fog.

Then her tittering kicked into a demented coughing and cackling. It was forced and it was finally no longer amused. She burst out of the fog real close to my face, and snarled, "Give me my mama's bones. And tell me how to use them."

I should have known that Tata Victor's relative silence up to now was a volcano waiting to explode. One second he was standing behind me, in his quiet but mountainous way, the next he had grabbed Alba by the throat and was thundering, "Why did you kill my boy, you little bitch?"

Alba simply let her little body go limp, dropping suddenly down against Victor's stomach. Victor lost his balance, and the girl pulled from inside her jacket what looked like a regular kitchen knife and stabbed Victor in the stomach. He loosened his grip and cursed as she tried to pull the knife out and wounded him worse. He gasped and snatched back his hands, and she scuttled back through the fog.

I thought I saw her dash behind a weeping willow.

Tata Victor cursed through his teeth, and from under where he was touching himself on his black T-shirt, I saw a wet circle getting wider.

I reached out a hand, but he yelled at me, "Go after her! I'll follow in a second. Let me catch my breath." He was breathing in big ragged gasps, and now I saw blood on his hands.

I could barely see where I was going. Sudden swimming wisps of fog.

A raccoon rose up on its hind legs, snarled at me and tried to bite my hand. I stepped back, and the animal slipped into the undergrowth. I tripped on the gnarled roots of a tree and bent over to steady myself. When I looked up, I saw a small tree that the wisps of fog, curling around its top trunk, turned into an ancient gnome.

Alba stepped from behind the tree and tore the plastic bag from my hands. She put the bloody kitchen knife to my throat.

"Don't move, Fina, or I'll stab you for true just like I did him."

"Alba, stop, it's not what you want."

I tried to look at her, and she grabbed the back of my neck with the hand holding the plastic bag and pressed me to her, digging fingers into my throat so that I started to choke. With the other hand she tapped with the knife at my neck.

"What?"

"That has my . . . my ancestor's remains in it. It's not your mother's bones."

"Where are they, Fina?"

"Victor has them now."

She slapped the bag against my body. "You better help me get my mother's bones. You know what I'll do to you."

"Alba, listen, do you remember, do you remember the beach?"

"Fuck you, Fina. I ain't got the time."

"Time? Time is what you need, don't you understand? You want me to tell you how to use your mother's bones? Don't you understand that can't be told or taught? Your mother didn't choose to give them to you. She chose me."

"I ain't chosen for that, huh? You know what I did to the last person who said that? I killed that fat little fuck! He tried to pull the same shit, said I couldn't keep my own mother's bones. He got his!"

Then, almost carelessly, she started scribbling with the knife on my throat. "How about this? You like this?"

They were light curlicues and zigzags that felt like damsel flies climbing up and down my skin. I swallowed and then tried to pull away slightly, and in the middle of my throat she dug the point of the knife in just a little deeper. I didn't feel pain, only a stronger sensation of insect pincers biting my throat.

When she leaned her face over my neck and kissed my cheek, my throat tightened.

I coughed. "Do you know why she chose me, Alba? Do you remember the beach?"

Still keeping her chokehold on my neck, she turned to face me and finally looked into my eyes. There was a glimmer of something, a thread of genuine feeling, like sunlight lancing through a swamp.

She cocked her head and looked away from me. She was trying to remember.

I jerked my neck away from the knife. Her eyes came back to me. She still had her hands on my neck, and the knife pressed to it, but she had stopped the carving on my throat.

"I remember a flash of . . . " She tilted her head. "Being on a beach. And floating out on the water. My mother grabbing me out of the water." She closed her eyes, shook her head. "I fucking don't remember her face. I fucking wish I could see her face some time before I die." She laughed shrilly. "But you say I ain't chosen."

I said softly, "There's a picture of her that Chico has. I'll get it for you."

She inclined her head slightly, her lips pressed together, and the knife point at my neck finally moved away.

"I had one of my visions, a beautiful vision. I saw her with you on a beach. I saw you as a baby, Alba."

"Yeah?" A little yearning there. Just a little.

"Yeah. You were a real ugly baby. Potbellied. Double-chinned. Only a mother could love you."

Alba opened her eyes wide and sliced at my face, but not before I managed to catch her wrist, twisted it and forced the knife in the opposite direction. Then with my other hand, I yanked it out of her hand and threw it off into the bushes.

"Fuck you, Fina! You catfood-cunted wannabe whitey witch. I'm gonna bite your ears off."

She flung herself on me and tried to bite me, so I rammed her forehead with mine.

There was a nice sharp crack, like a tree branch breaking and she screamed, "Let go of me," and sat down against the gnome tree, holding her head and rocking.

"I'm not going to hurt you, Alba."

Alba held her head in her hands and moaned a little. "You just fucking did, so you broke your promise before you even made it. That's why I can't promise you that I ain't gonna hurt you. I'm so good at it, you know? I do that better 'n anything. I even like it."

"Alba, that's just not true. The thing you do best is sing. You know that."

A snort, "So what good is that in the can? That ain't happening. I'm never going to jail. I'm running mad and madder."

I shook my head. "There are programs . . . "

"Stop it!" She threw up her hands. Then she brought a hand to her head again. "You know what I remember?"

I shook my head.

"Oh, God, I remember this." Her voice shook with excitement. "I remember loving that I was going out to sea. Out to infinity, just miles of ocean. And you know what else? *She* fucking pulled me back! My own mother. All my life, that's what it's been like. I been pulled back from infinity. I ain't been free. I ain't been given nothing. Even after I killed that poor stupid kid, I couldn't find the cauldron. She wouldn't let me see it. She wouldn't help me. I ain't never gonna float out free! That's why I gotta run now. Gotta try." She raised herself up into a crouch.

I got up quick and grabbed her by both shoulders and slammed her onto the ground. Then I proceeded to sit my big old body on top of hers.

"You listen to me." I held her shoulders, crushing her, like a refrigerator on top of a kitten. "You were an ugly baby, you crawled out from the sand like a crab. Then, you swam out to the ocean, 'cause you weren't afraid of nothing. Your mama went after you. You were ugly, but she put all these bright colored yellow and pink ribbons in your hair. She loved you like you were precious."

Alba's eyes watered and she closed them.

"You weren't afraid of jellyfish or sharks . . . or *anything*. That's what I saw," I said. "When did that change, Alba? When did you get so scared? So mean and scared?"

I heard quick running and strange murmuring sounds in the air—shedara shedara shedara—almost like the trees were murmuring around us: "she's there, she's there, she's there."

Alba's eyes widened darker than the darkness around us. "My mother taking me to the water . . . "

I saw the knife come up out of the fog, and I drew back, and jumped up. The ancient *munanso* knife with the big black blade and crude wooden handle. It chopped through Alba's throat.

Like the rooster's, her body jerked and flailed; and there was a deep clicking sound of death in her throat.

Victor pulled out the knife, and a thick jelly of blood seeped out of the deep gash in the girl's neck. The head flopped a bit to one side; because I felt it was about to fall off her neck, I reached out and tried to hold it in place, but it slipped out of my hands again and again. Finally, I let it fall.

I put out a hand, dropped to my knees and threw up right next to the body.

Through more and more breaks in the fog, I saw his shadowy face, spattered with blood.

He took out a length of brown cloth from a brown bag and wiped off the knife.

"I had to bring her down. Look at you, look at the fucking cuts on your neck. She was just going to keep on going. Evil as it gets."

I stood up and looked him in the face, but it was too dark and I couldn't see his eyes. "What about dark balancing the light? What about the tapestry of good and evil you're always talking about?"

Victor started wiping down his hands with the cloth. "There wasn't any light there. You saw it yourself. When you were *montada*. And I heard you tell her about it. She didn't understand, but I did. You saw that even her mother knew that the baby was bad."

The shallow knife cuts on my neck started to sting all at once, and I brought a hand to my throat, touched it and then looked at my hand. I couldn't see blood.

"There was some good in her. I could see it."

"No, Fina, you didn't see the good in her. You just saw what could have happened to you if you'd let your own losses twist you like that. It made you feel bad. What the hell has happened to you, woman? You think you're above killing, don't you? You think I take it lightly? I don't. I don't like killing, but it has to be done. I'm here to make sure the *Palo* traditions continue. There always has to be balance. And when you got an evil shit like this thing we called a girl running around, you gotta take care of it."

"If the cops come to ask me, I'm going to tell them that you killed her. Give me the bag with Aurora's bones. I'm not staying with you one more second. She had good in her. I could have helped her."

"I'll be long gone from here before the cops come sniffing around. I'm leaving New York. I'm leaving the States."

I slapped his face, and he just moved his head like a mosquito had landed on it. There was no anger in his eyes. I wanted to slap him again, but I sensed that he wanted that too. He wanted the contact, and I wasn't going to let him have it. "I can't believe you did this. I can't believe you won't be my *tata* any more. "

I could tell he was keeping a stone face on purpose. He touched the wound on his stomach, but kept looking into my eyes. But it was dark, and I couldn't see the burgundy lights in his eyes.

"I'm not angry with you." He held out the bag with the cauldron dirt and bones, and I could tell he wanted it to be a peace offering.

I snatched it from him. "This is mine. Don't think that because you're giving it freely it changes things. You're a killer now! You'll be on the run. How dare you make me a part of it! How could you dare to think I'd come with you?"

I turned my back on him, and he didn't follow.

Take us to the water . . .

The house in the water . . .

The horse to the house in the water . . .

I knelt next to the Pool, and closed my eyes. I thought of that ugly, double-chinned, potbellied baby riding the sand horse into the ocean of memory. The baby had wanted to munch on sand and float in seawater. The baby had sensed the sharks and the jellyfish, and had wanted to go to them. Natural, self-focused and in the moment, like an animal. Aurora had prettied up the ugly baby's hair in pink and yellow ribbons. How had Aurora, who'd not had much luck on the loving side, brought herself to love from the first a baby that she knew was bad?

I thought there was no answer, nothing left, other than my thought of a dream of a memory, which would lift away slowly, like the fog.

And the bones . . .

I seized both bags.

Rain came down hard, silver spikes, meeting and severing roots.

"*In the water. They die to live again, outside the bones.*"

I shook the contents of the plastic bags over the pool, and the bones sank into the water.

Up in the inkwell patch of sky, the moon came out from behind a cloud, and I watched the mass of dirt and bones spread right below the surface of the pool. Instead of spreading out even more, the darkness there on the surface of the water began to grow dense, a swirling darkness that seemed to collect itself into two shapes.

I thought I saw the outline of human bones, many more bones than I had thrown in there, floating, dancing and gathering together. And then a kind of gauzy skin hovered over the bones, and I saw their faces, and they spoke to me.

"*You are our daughter, come to us, come to us often, talk to us, name us, look at us. You are our daughter.*"

"Tell me what to do."

"*Name us. Make us real.*"

"Ángel. Aurora."

"*Call to us, make us your gods.*"

"Great-grandfather! Sister, mother!"

"*Become the horse, and raise the house. Name us, make us real.*"

"Aurora of the Park, goddess of water and dirt and blood. Father Darkness, god of time and bones, give me vision, give me sight and give me flight. Outside the bones!"

My spirit lifted high over the water, and I saw them staring up at me through the mirrored surface.

She was a woman of mud with blue and golden hair that streamed to the depths of the black water. I now remembered all of her journey, her past in the forest of memory, her striving towards the water. As I lifted higher in the air, I saw her shape in the water grow larger and fuller, moving to embrace the shape growing next to her.

I was still tied to my body and saw it kneeling and swaying dreamily next to the pool.

The male god in the water was darkness, a textured darkness of branches and bones, and plastic and rocks, balled fur and teeth and feathers, knives and guns and ice picks and every single hard thing that had ever been thrown into that murky water. And in that mass of darkness there were many eyes: the fierce eyes of my father, the burgundy depths of Victor's eyes when he still had the light in him, the cunt eye of Isis, the hollow sockets of the girl and all the dead, eyes watching as I watched.

No longer tied to the rituals and memories of the bones, I sped high over the quarried rock, the rustling trees, the coursing waters, the new gods and named spirits of my beloved Central Park.

GLOSSARY

Aché—strong spiritual energy, power and/or luck.

Botánica—a shop that sells herbs and other items for conjuring and religious purposes.

Bóveda—a kind of spiritual altar composed of seven to nine glasses filled with water on a weekly basis and honoring the spirits of the dead in a particular family.

Cocolo—a complex term often used in Puerto Rico to refer to people who live in the housing projects; it can also be used out of context, and derogatorily, to designate vulgarity.

Despojo—a cleansing ritual.

Fufú—a spell; *echar un fufú*, cast a spell.

"La sangre llama"—"blood calls."

Madre de Agua—*Palo* goddess or *nkisi* associated with the ocean and motherhood. She is often also identified with the *Santería orisha Yemayá*.

Mama Chola—*Palo* goddess or *nkisi* associated with river water and a more forward kind of sexuality. She is also often identified with the *Santería orisha Oshún*.

Mayombe—of the forest or the bush.

Montada—possessed by an *nkisi*, *nfuiri* or other spirit.

Moriviví—*Mimosa pudica*, a tiny perennial, also called the Sensitive Plant. Its leaves fold inward when touched. In Puerto Rico, the name "moriviví" literally means "to die/to live."

Mpungo (plural *Kimpungulu*)—another word for *nkisi* or *Palo* deity.

Munanso—a particular "house," temple or group led by a *palero*.

Nfuiri—a commandeered spirit, usually inhabiting a cauldron, who specifically follows the orders of the *palero* who "made" it and keeps it bound to the cauldron.

Nganga—in *Palo* the *nganga* is the iron pot or cauldron that houses a spirit; the term can also sometimes refer to the spirit residing in the cauldron.

Nkisis—ancestral or pantheon deities; some of them are also syncretized with Catholic saints. The term can also refer to spirits of water and woods.

Nkuyo—messenger deity of woods and roads, guidance and balance.

Nsambia—the supreme deity of *Palo* who rules over the other *nkisis*, the universe and the dead.

Orishas—the gods of another Afro-Caribbean religion called *Santería*; as in *Palo*, they are also identified, or syncretized, with Catholic saints. For example, in *Santería*, Saint Barbara (Santa Bárbara) and the deity *Changó* are one and the same.

Palo—an Afro-Caribbean religio-magical tradition derived from the Bantu spiritual systems of West Central Africa in which conjuring is done with *palos*, wooden sticks or tree branches, in cauldrons and other receptacles. First formed to resist slavery in colonial Cuba, it incorporated indigenous Taíno and European elements in its Criollo/Creole veneration of the ancestors, the dead and nature in general, with several branches and lines of the tradition spread the world over to New York, Miami and Puerto Rico, among other places.

Siete Rayos—the *Palo nkisi* or deity who rules over thunder, fire and divine justice. When he is painted or represented, he often appears as an *esclavo cimarrón*, a runaway slave who has escaped to the bush; or he is identified with the Catholic Saint Barbara, who also wears red robes. He is often also syncretized with the *Santería orisha Changó*.

Yemayá—*Santería orisha* and deity of the ocean and motherhood; she is often identified with the *Palo nkisi* or goddess Madre de Agua.

Tata—a *Palo* priest or trained specialist in magic and divination. The title means roughly "Papá" because the *Tata* is the father of his *munanso* and of all whom he initiates and advises.

Zarabanda—the *Palo nkisi* or deity of iron, war and sorcery. He is often identified with the *Santería orisha Ogún*.

ACKNOWLEDGEMENTS

I am grateful for a sabbatical leave from the City College of New York, without which I would not have been able to write this book. I am also thankful for strong support from the PSC-CUNY Research Foundation. I am indebted to Tata Candela Entierra's real-life and boundless knowledge of *Palo,* his generosity and loving kindness, as well as that of his *munanso.* Michael Martin read an early version of the manuscript in its entirety, and provided helpful comments. My dear friends Hermann Ferré, Paul Leslie, Diane Mehta, Professor Richard Perez and Emérida Rivera provided needed input on myriad details and did so with alacrity. I am grateful for Missy Yearian's lucidity and dynamic energy regarding countless book-related matters. Wilfred Santiago created the cover art according to my description of Aurora and the *ngangas,* and I thank my agent Mark McVeigh for facilitating that process and for his kindness. Nicolás Kanellos showed enthusiasm for this project, and I am grateful to all the staff at Arte Público for their hard work on it, especially Marina Tristán and Gabriela Baeza Ventura. As a young girl growing up in Puerto Rico, I was particularly delighted to discover the fiction of Rosario Ferré, Jean Rhys and Ana Lydia Vega. Their diverse engagements with literature, popular culture, politics and Caribbean identity, were formative to my sensibility and instruct the tone of this book. The talking skull, in Chapter Three, was inspired by a passage in Lydia Cabrera's seminal book, *El Monte.* The hundreds of students I've worked with at The City College of New York and more recently at CUNY Graduate Center have taught me a great deal about deploying and combining sophistication and street savviness, and I tried to convey a bit of that in Fina Mata. Honey Betancourt, in particular, opened my eyes to the practice of Afro-Caribbean religions in New York. Special thanks to my beloved husband, Xavier Romeu Matta, for reading the many drafts, past, present and to come! My mother, Esther Sandín de Di Iorio, has forgotten much, but not what is essential. Her love continues to illuminate my life.